SAVING CAMELOT

A Screenplay

Marvin J. Wolf and Larry Mintz

Rambam Press
Los Angeles, California

This is a work of fiction. All of the characters, organizations, and events portrayed in this novel are either products of the author's imagination or are used fictitiously.

SAVING CAMELOT. Copyright © 2013 by Marvin Wolf and Larry Mintz. All rights reserved. For information, address Rambam Press, 13237 Warren Avenue, Los Angeles CA 90066

Library of Congress Cataloging-in-Publication Data

Wolf, Marvin and Mintz, Larry
  Saving Camelot / Marvin Wolf and Larry Mintz
    p. cm.
   ISBN 978-0-9899600-1-4

Time travel—screenplay. 2. Dallas (Texas)—Fiction. I. Title

FADE IN:

EXT. AEGEAN SEA, LAST YEAR - DAY.

Two women sunbathe on the deck of a CABIN CRUISER gently bobbing on a picture-postcard sea.

EXT. SEA BENEATH CABIN CRUISER - DAY

Two SCUBA DIVERS cruise clear water near a white sand bottom.

Suddenly ONE GESTURES, then TURNS. The other FOLLOWS.

EXT. SEABED, SCUBA DIVERS' P.O.V. - DAY

Covered by BARNACLES, the PROW of an ancient Roman ship.

Scattered nearby on the seabed are dozens of AMPHORAE.

EXT. CALIFORNIA INSTITUTE OF TECHNOLOGY, PRESENT DAY - DAY

To establish.

INT. CAL TECH CLASSROOM - DAY

A PACKED CLASSROOM of casually dressed STUDENTS.

On walls are POSTERS of ANCIENT ENGINEERING WONDERS: Egypt's pyramids, Stonehenge, Mesopotamian ziggurats (stepped pyramids), the Great Wall of China, and line drawings of several MYSTERIOUS DEVICES.

PROF. ROBERT GODWIN, vigorous 60s, chinos, blazer, open-neck Oxford shirt, LIGHTS a BUNSEN BURNER under a melon-sized copper SPHERE on a PIPE STAND over a KETTLE. PIPES connect the kettle with the sphere. Stubby, L-shaped pipes protrude from OPPOSITE SIDES of the sphere.

                    GODWIN

          Good morning. Those of you on athletic
          scholarships and looking for an easy "A," I
          suggest you try Quantum Mechanics. Next door.

The students CHUCKLE.

GODWIN (CONT'D)
What's an engineer?

A STUDENT raises his hand. Godwin NODS.

STUDENT
Engineers build stuff.

SEPIA -- NO AUDIO

INT. OHIO APARTMENT, 1955 - DAY

Godwin as BOY of 5 watches his DAD, 40s, at drafting table.

INT. CAL TECH CLASSROOM - DAY

GODWIN
Good! Engineers create *artifacts*. And they all
stand on the shoulders of those who went before
them. For example: One guy invents a wheel.
Then someone joins two wheels with an axle.
Then along comes the cart. Then an engine...
This goes on until someone invents the freeway.
Then everything stops.

The students LAUGH. Then they SEE the copper sphere over the burner is
SPINNING. STEAM comes from the L-shaped pipes.

GODWIN (CONT'D)
Ladies and gentlemen, I give you the steam
engine. Invented by who?

A cute ASIAN COED raises her hand and RISES when Godwin nods.

ASIAN COED
James Watt? In 1765?

GODWIN
(Makes noise like game show BUZZER)
Anyone else?

The room is QUIET.

                    GODWIN (CONT'D)
          This is called an aeolipile. Invented by Hero, a
          Greek living in Alexandria -- about 40 C.E.
          (BEAT)
          Who here has an iPad?

EVERY hand in the room goes up.

                    GODWIN (CONT'D)
          It requires a battery. So, when did *those* first
          come along?

A BLACK TEENAGER stands up.

                    BLACK TEENAGER
          Invented by Alessandro Volta, 1800.

                    GODWIN
          (Noise like game show buzzer) In 1936, while
          excavating 2,000-year-old ruins near Baghdad...

He POINTS to a POSTER of a ceramic vase.

                    GODWIN (CONT'D)
          ...workers discovered a yellow vase six inches
          high. Inside was a cylinder of sheet copper. Its
          bottom was capped with a crimped copper disk.
          Top and bottom were sealed with asphalt.

          An iron rod was suspended in the center of the
          copper cylinder. When filled with vinegar or
          lemon juice, the vase produced one volt of
          electricity.

The students are AMAZED.

                    GODWIN (CONT'D)
          We're still not sure what they used it for. But we
          know this: science tells us how nature behaves,
          but engineers always have a purpose in mind for
          anything they build....

EXT. CALTECH IMAGING LAB - DAY

A low-slung, futuristic building.

INT. CALTECH IMAGING LAB

Godwin watches a LAB-COATED TECHNICIAN and BILL, 20s, a GRAD
STUDENT, unpack a large wooden crate with GREEK LETTERS. They remove
layers of padding to reveal a four-foot-long, BARNACLE ENCRUSTED amphora.
One man grabs either end.

> GODWIN
> Careful! It's over 2,000 years old!

> BILL
> It's a lot bigger than the ones we saw on our
> field trip.

> GODWIN
> There were millions of amphorae -- the shipping
> container of choice for the ancient world. Wine,
> honey, olive oil, grain, dates --

> TECHNICIAN
> I feel something sloshing inside.

Gently, they place it in a CT machine.

> GODWIN
> Gentlemen, we're in for a treat.

Godwin opens an ENVELOPE to get a fuzzy ULTRASOUND IMAGE. He shows it
to the technician and to Bill.

> GODWIN (CONT'D)
> Ultrasound from Dr. Bitsakis at the Greek
> National Museum. This was recovered from a
> shipwreck off Rhodes.
>
> Looks like a wine amphora with a secret
> compartment holding two objects. With your
> help, I'm going to try to identify them.

> TECHNICIAN
> Piece of cake, Professor.

Int. Control booth - DAY

Behind a huge window overlooking the CT machine, is a big imaging screen
surrounded by controls.

The technician pushes a button and the WHINE of machinery is heard. They watch as the amphora SLIDES into the scanner.

> TECHNICIAN
> First, we'll look under the barnacles for cracks
> or markings.

ON THE SCREEN

Layers of pocked barnacle and limestone are magically peeled away. The outlines of the original amphora appear. On its PALE ROSE surface is a PAINTING of a buxom, bare-busted maiden with a large amphora on her shoulder.

> GODWIN
> Hebe, Goddess of Youth.

> BILL
> Roman?

> GODWIN
> Greek. Amazing detail!

> TECHNICIAN
> Say, doc, weren't you one of the guys who
> developed CT technology?

SEPIA -- NO AUDIO

INT. HIGH SCHOOL CLASSROOM, 1962 - DAY

Wearing drab school uniform, Godwin at AGE 16 sits in front row as teacher lectures. A picture of JFK is on the wall.

INT. CALTECH IMAGING LAB - DAY

> GODWIN
> I was on that team...for awhile.

> BILL
> Then you shared in their Patzger Prize?

                    GODWIN
          I had to leave the project before the big
          breakthrough.

Off a LOOK by Bill

                    GODWIN (CONT'D)
          I was offered tenure here. I had student loans, a
          fiancée to consider.

                    TECHNICIAN
          I didn't know you were married.

SEPIA -- NO AUDIO

INT. HIGH SCHOOL LIBRARY, 1962 - DAY

**In school uniform, Godwin AGE 16 studies with a GIRL with LONG
DARK HAIR and HUGE EYES. They hold hands under table.**

**The girl has become a dark-haired YOUNG WOMAN with huge eyes
RECLINING in a HAMMOCK on a summer day.**

The young woman is pale, tired-looking.

The woman lies still in a HOSPITAL BED connected to machines.

INT. CALTECH IMAGING LAB - DAY

                    GODWIN
          How long's this gonna take?

                    TECHNICIAN
          Give me a few hours and I'll peel this puppy like
          an onion.

                    GODWIN
          I'll be back.

INT. CALTECH, GODWIN'S OFFICE - NIGHT

An INVITING SPACE: Easy chair and desk, comfy sofa.

On the desk a large, ornate CIGAR HUMIDOR.

FRESHLY-PAINTED LIGHT BLUE walls are bare. Pictures, framed diplomas, awards, etcetera, are stacked NEATLY in corners. Furniture and bookcases are pulled away from the walls.

Godwin sits at his computer. On the monitor are dozens of CT IMAGES of the amphora and its CONTENTS. In the corner of the screen is a WEBCAM image of a BEAMING NICO BITSAKIS, 50s.

> GODWIN
> Nico! It's two in the morning. How did you know
> I'd be here?

> BITSAKIS
> How could anyone sleep after seeing these
> images!

ANGLE SCREEN

A SERIES OF THREE-DIMENSIONAL COLOR IMAGES:

A top-to-bottom vertical section of the amphora showing a secret compartment.

The compartment containing a small, tear-shaped object and a larger, box-like object, both SHROUDED in white.

A full view of the tear-shaped object.

> BITSAKIS (O.C.)
> What a find! A Baghdad Battery!

A full length picture of a YELLOW CERAMIC VASE with an IRON ROD sticking out of either end.

A top-to-bottom sequence of three-dimensional slices of the amphora showing a central iron rod and copper sheath.

ANGLE GODWIN AT THE COMPUTER

> GODWIN
> The last thing I expected!

> BITSAKIS
> You have no idea what this will mean to Greece!
> (softly) And to our funding.

ANGLE SCREEN

A NEW SERIES OF THREE-DIMENSIONAL COLOR IMAGES:

A full-length view of an unadorned wooden CABINET.

Layer by layer, like peeling an onion, innards are revealed:

A dial adorned with images of Greek gods

A succession of GEARED WHEELS, DIALS and ODD OBJECTS.

An INTRICATE COMPLEX OF tiny metal ASSEMBLAGES

                    GODWIN (O.C.)
            What do you make of all this, Nico?

A BIG PIECE of AMBER surrounding TINY bronze assemblages

A slab of wood -- the back of the cabinet.

                    BITSAKIS (O.C.)
            You're the engineer.

Layered images are MERGED, revealing a detailed view of a rectangular, shoe-box sized device that RESEMBLES a clock.

                    GODWIN (O.C.)
            At first I thought it was a version of the
            Antikythera Mechanism -- an analog computer
            for navigation at sea. But this is far more
            complex.

            It speaks to a sophistication far beyond what we
            know of ancient Greece. I might get some
            answers if you'll allow me to examine the actual
            device.

ANGLE GODWIN AT THE COMPUTER

                    BITSAKIS
            Now *I* won't be able to sleep.

INT. HISTORY DEPARTMENT CONFERENCE ROOM - DAY

Around the table are DAN SULLIVAN, 45, LYNDA MARKS, 37, SINGH RAY, 30, and Godwin, FIDGETING in his seat.

                    RAY
          You Americans! You start a war, find you've
          bitten off more than you can chew -- and when
          the papers report setbacks, your government
          blames everything on the media!

                    MARKS
          Do we *really* have to fight the War of 1812
          again?

                    GODWIN
          (clears throat) I have some work I'd really like
          to get back to. Can you get along without me
          today?

                    SULLIVAN
          I don't see why not. We're only discussing
          Thornley's dissertation.

                    MARKS
          He postulates that assassins influenced history
          to a greater degree than did their victims.

                    GODWIN
          I'll read it.

Robert opens the door to leave and MIKE THORNLEY, 24, enters.

                    THORNLEY
          Is this the dissertation committee?

                    GODWIN
          Come in Mr. Thornley. We've been sharpening
          our instruments.

INT. CALTECH MECHANICAL ENGINEERING LAB - DAY

Wearing gloves and an apron, Godwin and Bill stand at a lab table. Before them are the empty cocoon of beeswax and leather, and the DEVICE. Godwin stares at the bronze GEARS, WHEELS and DIALS with a look of wonder. He EYES two protruding rods on the SIDE of the device.

Godwin beckons to Bill and they sit at a computer screen showing a finely-woven matrix pattern of lines and spaces.

                    GODWIN
          What's this look like to you?

Bill peers closely at the screen.

                    BILL
          Some kinda micro circuit?

                    GODWIN
          On a 2,100 year old artifact?

                    BILL
          Yeah. Can't be that. Beats me.

                    GODWIN
          Me too.

INT. CALTECH, GODWIN'S OFFICE - NIGHT

Godwin ADMIRES the device. He runs his fingers over it, then pauses, frowning.

Godwin turns to his computer and brings up IMAGES of the Baghdad Battery. He zooms the screen and finds two metal studs, top and bottom. Using a VIRTUAL RULER, he measures the distance between them.

With a wooden ruler he measures the gap between the bronze rods on the side of the device: THEY MATCH. Godwin is AMAZED.

Godwin gets up and paces around his office, lost in thought. Abruptly he opens a cabinet and comes out with an OLD 35mm CAMERA. He TURNS IT OVER and opens the battery compartment, then PRIES a reluctant battery out with a letter opener.

The tiny battery is GREEN with corrosion.

                    GODWIN
          Great.

EXT. CAMERA STORE - MORNING

Godwin gets into his restored 1961 Porsche 356 Cabriolet.

Lighting a CIGAR, he pulls out into traffic.

EXT. CALIFORNIA STREET, PASADENA - DAY

Godwin STOPS to allow a gaggle of SCHOOL KIDS to cross. The 70-ish
CROSSING GUARD SMILES at Godwin as she waves him on.

As he turns onto California Street, Godwin passes a BOOK STORE just as a
clerk wheels a BIN of BARGAIN BOOKS out.

The Porsche approaches the corner of Lake Street; distracted by a GORGEOUS
WOMAN on a bus bench, Godwin runs the light.

In the next block a motorcycle COP stops him.

INT. GODWIN'S OFFICE - DAY

Dropping a bag on his desk, Godwin throws the TRAFFIC TICKET down with
disgust. He takes a small screwdriver from his desk drawer and begins to
disassemble the camera.

INT. GODWIN'S OFFICE - LATER

Godwin extracts a tiny BATTERY from the bag. He lays the Device on its side,
revealing a jury-rigged battery compartment salvaged from the camera and
TAPED to the wooden cabinet. He inserts the battery.

Muttering to himself, he inspects the Device closely and begins to FIDDLE with
it. He pushes a tiny lever. He moves a gear one way, then another. He pushes
the lever AGAIN.

SFX: The scene SHIMMERS, WARPS, then FREEZES.

COLOR DRAINS to SEPIA, then to OVEREXPOSED monochrome WASH.

COLOR FLOODS IN TO OVERSATURATE the image, fading to NORMAL.

Godwin sits on the floor next to his overturned chair, back against a wall. A
framed photo behind SHATTERED glass lies on the floor nearby. Blood trickles
from a cut on his FOREHEAD.

Taking a PRESCRIPTION VIAL from a pocket, Godwin puts a tablet under his
tongue. He staggers to his feet.

INT. MENS ROOM - DAY

Godwin WASHES the cut on his forehead as Thornley enters.

                    THORNLEY
          Professor Godwin! You okay?

                    GODWIN
          Just a scratch. A picture frame that fell off my
          office wa--

A LOOK of BEWILDERMENT passes over his face.

                    THORNLEY
          Professor?

                    GODWIN
          (covering) Good to see you, Thornley. Great job
          on your dissertation.

                    THORNLEY
          (confused) My dissertation? It's not due until
          next week.

                    GODWIN
          Well, people are already raving about it. Please
          excuse me.

INT. GODWIN'S OFFICE - DAY

Godwin STANDS in the center of the room.

He SEES the walls are DIRTY BEIGE and covered with framed photos and
memorabilia.

                    GODWIN
          No. No. This *can't* be.

He rights his chair and sits down, thinking.

He glances at his digital WATCH, which reads JAN 9.

                    GODWIN (CONT'D)
          But that was 11 days ago.

At the computer he clicks CLOCK/CALENDAR. It reads JAN 9th.

> GODWIN (CONT'D)
> No way.

He LOOKS OUT HIS WINDOW, thinking. Abruptly he picks up the phone and dials a number.

> GODWIN (CONT'D)
> What's today's date?
> (BEAT)
> Are you certain?

He hangs up.

> GODWIN (CONT'D)
> Think, Robert Godwin. *Think.*

He looks around and finds the Device lying on the floor. The BATTERY COMPARTMENT is AJAR and the battery is GONE.

On hands and knees he searches until he finds the battery under a chair. He starts to replace it, then STOPS.

He puts the battery on the desk, places the Device next to it, and carefully opens the case.

With the tip of a letter opener, he probes the wheels looking for clues as to their function.

He tries the gear wheel that he touched earlier and discovers that it moves one click at a time.

When he MOVES the second wheel ONE click, the first WHEEL QUICKLY ROTATES almost a complete circle.

> GODWIN (CONT'D)
> (mumbles) That's *months.* So this must be *days.*

He gets up and paces the room. Then he sits down, returns the gears to their previous positions. Puts the battery in, moves the first wheel, COUNTING OUT LOUD.

> GODWIN (CONT'D)
> January 10, 11, 12, 13, 14, 15, 16, 17, 18, 19
> and 20.

The Device in his lap, he sits against the wall. He replaces the battery and gingerly presses the lever.

(BEAT)

He presses it again.

SFX: The scene SHIMMERS, WARPS, then FREEZES.

COLOR DRAINS to SEPIA, then to OVEREXPOSED monochrome WASH.

COLOR FLOODS IN TO OVERSATURATE the image, fading to NORMAL.

Godwin slowly STANDS and looks around. He sees fresh paint on bare walls, piles of books and personal memorabilia.

He touches his forehead: The cut is still fresh. Slowly he BRINGS HIS WATCH UP and LOOKS at the date.

Slowly, he SHAKES HIS HEAD in DISBELIEF. He knows what has happened, but he's not ready to accept it.

EXT. CALTECH CAMPUS - DAY

In a daze, Godwin strolls along the sunlit quad.

PROFESSOR WOLFGANG WIEMAN, spry 70s, stops him.

> WIEMAN
> Robert?

Godwin stares UNCOMPREHENDING at Wieman.

> WIEMAN (CONT'D)
> Are you all right?

> GODWIN
> Oh hello, Wolfie!

> WIEMAN
> Have you forgotten our lunch?

INT. FACULTY DINING ROOM, "THE ATHENAEUM CLUB" - DAY

An upscale private club for faculty.

Godwin and Wieman regard each other across a table.

                    WIEMAN
So now the absent-minded professor?

                    GODWIN
(grunt) I'm thinking about a novel.

A WAITER arrives.

                    WAITER
Have you gentlemen decided?

                    WIEMAN
How does the '99 Burrweiler Schawer sound?

Godwin SHRUGS and the waiter hurries off.

                WIEMAN (CONT'D)
A novel? You waste your time reading escape
literature?

                    GODWIN
I'm thinking about *writing* one.

                    WIEMAN
Please, not another manipulative professor who
sleeps with students.

                    GODWIN
It's about a journey through time.

Off Wieman's SKEPTICAL LOOK.

                GODWIN (CONT'D)
Some scholars believe that the Egyptians saw
the pyramids not merely as tombs but as
vehicles to reach the future.

And Hunsackler posits that Homer's Iliad and
Odyssey allude to travels through time as well as
space.

So, as the only Nobel Prize-winning physicist
that I know, tell me: Is time travel theoretically
possible?

                    WIEMAN
We should have had *dinner!* Forty years ago, I
would have said that time travel is science
fiction. But in the last two decades or so we've
learned how little we truly know.
(BEAT)
Now, very serious physicists are publishing
theories about "worm holes" through multiple
dimensions, about instant travel to galaxies
millions of light years away.

                    GODWIN
So it could be possible?

                    WIEMAN
Who am I to argue with my elders?

                    GODWIN
What if my novel's protagonist goes back in time
to assassinate Hitler?

                    WIEMAN
At first, Hitler was only a figurehead. Kill him
and the Nazis find someone else. It would seem
far more noble if your character *stopped* an
assassination.

                    GODWIN
That's interesting. Yes.

                    WIEMAN
But complicated. What if McKinley wasn't shot?
Would Theodore Roosevelt ever become
President?

SEPIA -- NO AUDIO

INT. HIGH SCHOOL CLASSROOM, 1962 - DAY

**Godwin at AGE 16 sits in front row as door opens and PRINCIPAL
ENTERS. He WHISPERS TO TEACHER.**

                                        JUMP CUT TO:

INT. FACULTY DINING ROOM, "THE ATHENAEUM CLUB" - DAY

                    GODWIN
          But what would the world would be like now if
          Kennedy had lived?

          I remember that day. I was 16.

SEPIA -- NO AUDIO

INT. HIGH SCHOOL CLASSROOM, 1962 - DAY

HEAD IN HAND, the TEACHER WEEPS as SHOCKED-LOOKING students
somberly file out of the room. Most are crying.

INT. FACULTY DINING ROOM,"THE ATHENAEUM CLUB" - DAY

                    WIEMAN
          JFK was the reason that I came to America.
          Kennedy made being a pointy-head intellectual
          sexy. And for that, I'll be forever grateful.

          But Robert, a novel? An over-educated Stanley
          Kowalski contemplating old age, wondering why
          he was never a contender?

                    GODWIN
          It's true. I had my chances, and I didn't climb
          into the ring. I left it to others to change the
          world.

                    WIEMAN
          Teachers change the world every day, Robert.
          Look at how many of your students have gone
          on to brilliant careers. Two were nominated for
          a Nobel Prize!

                    GODWIN
          If they'd taken Kerr's class instead of mine,
          wouldn't they still have been nominated? Who
          knows, maybe they would have won?

          I had my golden opportunity, a lottery ticket for
          fame and fortune. But I played it safe, went with
          the sure thing. And now...

                              WIEMAN
            Robert! Regret is a cancer! What's done is done.
            Look to the future, not to the past. Where's our
            waiter with the wine?

EXT. GODWIN'S HOUSE - DAY

To establish

A modest three-bedroom tract home in a Pasadena canyon. Lawns are
immaculately manicured. The house is freshly painted.

Godwin's Porsche cabriolet is in the driveway.

INT. GODWIN'S HOUSE - DAY

In slippers and a robe, Godwin enters the kitchen and fills a glass with
ORANGE JUICE from the refrigerator. He SEES the TRAFFIC TICKET under a
fridge door magnet and SCOWLS.

SEPIA -- NO AUDIO

INT. HIGH SCHOOL CLASSROOM, 1962 - DAY

Godwin, 16, watches PRINCIPAL SPANK a student with a PADDLE.

INT. GODWINS'S HOUSE MASTER BED ROOM - DAY

An IMMACULATE space organized with near MILITARY PRECISION.

Fully dressed, Godwin pulls the bedding off the bed. He drags the mattress to
the wall beneath the window.

Clutching the Device, Godwin sits against the mattress. Carefully he ROTATES
the gears and pushes the lever TWICE.

SFX: Godwin moves back through time

Godwin sits against the wall, rubbing the back of his head, grimacing. Looking
at the perfectly-made bed, he grins.

EXT. PASADENA STREET - DAY

As before, Godwin drives his Porsche, puffing a large cigar.

Godwin STOPS to allow the gaggle of SCHOOL KIDS to cross the street. The CROSSING GUARD SMILES at Godwin, waves him on.

As he turns onto California street, Godwin passes a BOOK STORE just as the clerk wheels a BIN of BARGAIN BOOKS out.

As the light turns YELLOW, Godwin approaches the corner and SPOTS the same beauty on the bench. He BRAKES to a halt.

TORTURED TIRES BURN and SCREAM!

A CRUNCH OF sheet metal!

Godwin's Porsche is REAR ENDED!

Godwin looks in the rearview mirror and sees the IRATE driver of a BATTERED pickup truck getting out of his vehicle.

> PICKUP DRIVER
> Look what you done to my truck!
> Why the hell did you stop for? Now we got to
> wait for the cops!

> GODWIN
> (points) There -- in the alley.

The driver SQUINTS into the distance.

> PICKUP DRIVER
> Damn! You got good eyes, buddy.

INT. GODWINS'S BEDROOM - DAY

Godwin sits in front of the wall. The bed is MADE.

He fiddles with the Device. Pushes the lever. Again.

SFX: GODWIN MOVES BACK THROUGH TIME

Godwin sits against the mattress, smiling.

INT. GODWIN'S HOUSE, KITCHEN - DAY

Godwin looks at the refrigerator. The TRAFFIC TICKET is GONE.

He SMILES.

Then he LOOKS outside and SEES his car's smashed rear end.

> GODWIN
> (mutters) I *can* change history. But not
> necessarily for the better.

INT. GODWIN'S OFFICE - NIGHT

Godwin has Bitsakis in his webcam window.

> GODWIN
> Nico, you've seen the images, so you know that
> the Device has all sorts of calendar references
> on those dials. Now I should convert the old
> Metonic calendar to our present system.

> BITSAKIS
> I'll e-mail you a program that I wrote for quick
> conversions. But it could be off as much as one
> percent, plus or minus.
> (BEAT)
> Nothing you can share now?

> GODWIN
> (covering) Nothing for sure. I'll get back to you
> when I know more.

INT. CALTECH LIBRARY - DAY

Godwin sits at a study carrel, surrounded by books and magazines, reading a
1963 "Dallas Morning News" on MICROFILM.

On the desk is a copy of "The Warren Commission Report."

He turns off the microfilm reader and begins to leaf through the pages of a
1963 "Esquire Magazine." He pauses at an ad for a 1963 Porsche, chuckling
over its list price of $5,325.

He flips pages, looking at ads, until he finds a Brooks Brothers ad. On the
other page a Camel Cigarette ad claims that "More Doctors Smoke Camels Than
Any Other Cigarette."

EXT. BLANCHARD AND COMPANY, COIN DEALERS - DAY

To establish.

INT. BLANCHARD AND COMPANY, COIN DEALERS - DAY

Godwin watches a CLERK spread money on a counter.

> CLERK
> Our entire inventory, sir. Eleven thousand, five
> hundred, two dollars in pre-1964 U.S. currency.
>
> Ones, fives, tens, twenties and fifties. That
> comes to $28,409.

Godwin hands him a AMERICAN EXPRESS CARD.

> CLERK (CONT'D)
> An investment?

> GODWIN
> More like a hedge.

MONTAGE:

Godwin leaving MONTGOMERY COIN & CURRENCY.

Godwin standing at counter in LEFEBRE'S COLLECTIBLES

Godwin entering SILVER LAKE COINS AND BULLION.

EXT. TAYLOR'S VINTAGE CLOTHES - DAY

Robert comes out of a trendy Melrose used clothing store carrying an OLD
SUITCASE and a GARMENT BAG.

INT. GODWIN'S CALTECH OFFICE - DAY

Sitting at his computer and referring to the Warren Commission Report for
names and addresses, Godwin WRITES and PRINTS OUT letters to the Secret
Service, the FBI, CIA, Dallas Police, Texas Department of Public Safety,
President Kennedy, and Texas Governor John Connally:

DO NOT ALLOW PRESIDENT KENNEDY OR
GOVERNOR CONNALLY TO VISIT DALLAS ON
NOVEMBER 22. LEE HARVEY OSWALD, A
FORMER MARINE SHARPSHOOTER, HAS A BOLT
ACTION, MAIL-ORDER RIFLE AND INTENDS TO
KILL THEM AS THEIR CAR PASSES THE TEXAS
BOOK DEPOSITORY.

OSWALD USES ALIASES ALEK HIDELL AND O. H.
LEE. HE LIVES AT 1026 N. BECKLEY AVE,
DALLAS, A BOARDING HOUSE.

HIS MANNLICHER CARCANO RIFLE IS HIDDEN IN
THE GARAGE OF RUTH PAINE IN IRVING, TEXAS,
WHERE HIS WIFE, MARINA, RESIDES.

He puts the first LETTER in an envelope.

EXT. SAN ANTONIO AIRPORT - DAY

To establish.

INT. SAN ANTONIO AIRPORT MEN'S ROOM - DAY

Godwin puts his cell phone, digital watch, wallet and keys into his briefcase.
He starts to UNDRESS.

INT. SAN ANTONIO AIRPORT "LEFT LUGGAGE" ROOM - DAY

In vintage Sixties garb, Godwin pockets a claim check.

EXT. ALAMO PARK, SAN ANTONIO - DAY

Godwin SITS on the grass near the ALAMO He takes the Device from the shopping bag, EYES people walking dogs, kids playing, picnickers, etc. Nobody pays him any attention.

Carefully, he positions the gears. He inserts the BATTERY.

He closes his eyes and pushes the lever. And again.

SFX: GODWIN MOVES BACK THROUGH TIME

The rattle of small arms fire competes with louder blasts from cannons.

GODWIN'S P.O.V. - DAY

The air is filled with GUN SMOKE and the ROAR of CANNON.

Horses dash by dragging a NAPOLEONEC ERA CANNON on a carriage.

Right behind trot dozens of MEXICAN SOLDIERS in ORNATE BLUE uniforms with RED caps and WHITE belts.

SERGEANTS BARK ORDERS. The soldiers FORM RANKS, FIRE muskets.

More big guns are dragged into position and loaded by bare-chested crews. On SHOUTED COMMANDS they BELCH fire.

A contingent of MEXICAN CAVALRY rides by only 100 yards away.

Suddenly fair-skinned MEN in buckskin appear out of the bushes near Godwin. They fire long-barreled RIFLES at the Mexicans. Some of the Mexicans FALL. Others return fire.

                         FRONTIERSMAN (O.C.)
                 You! Boy! Get the hell out of here!

EXT. ALAMO PARK - DAY

A SKINNY, SHORT and BEWILDERED TEENAGED BOY SWIMS in GODWIN'S MAN-SIZED SIXTIES CLOTHES. The BATTLE RAGES ON AROUND HIM.

A BIG frontiersman TUCKS the boy under one arm, GRABS the Device and the suitcase and rushes off.

INT. ALAMO, GROUND-FLOOR OFFICE - DAY

A ROTARY TELEPHONE on an OLD WOODEN DESK. A SAFE. A MANUAL TYPEWRITER. A CALENDAR that SAYS JUNE 1963.

                    GODWIN
          (relieved) Thank God!

PUGH, a burly PARK POLICEMAN, goes through Godwin's suitcase.

                    PUGH
          You stole them re-enactors clothes?

                    GODWIN
          Hell no! And that's *my* suitcase.

The cop holds up a PILL VIAL and a GILLETTE DOUBLE-EDGED RAZOR and gets in Godwin's face.

                    PUGH
          Whatcha doing with heart medicine? And when
          did *you* start shaving?

                    GODWIN
          While we're on the subject of personal hygiene,
          have you ever heard of soap?

                    PUGH
          Show a little respect, boy.

The cop turns to the Device.

                    PUGH (CONT'D)
          This come outta the museum?

Godwin shakes his head, DISGUSTED.

The cop pulls a sheaf of ENVELOPES out of the bag.

                    PUGH (CONT'D)
          (READING) FBI, Secret Service, Texas Rangers,
          Dallas Police --

The cop drops the envelopes in the suitcase, snaps it shut.

PUGH (CONT'D)
Don't you move a muscle.

Taking the suitcase, Pugh locks the door behind him.

In a corner of the office is a sink and a MIRROR. Godwin drags a chair over and stands on it, peers into the mirror.

GODWIN
My God! I'm a kid...again!

He hops down and grabs the Device. He TRIPS on his trouser legs and DROPS the device.

The battery pops out and ROLLS under a massive steel SAFE.

Godwin grabs a RULER off the desk and fishes around under the safe. No luck.

He starts to roll his pant cuffs.

INT. THE ALAMO - DAY

Pugh and Sergeant HINES, bigger, walk down a corridor.

PUGH
Them re-enactor boys grabbed him up when he
was making off with a clock he stole. Got a
mouth on him -- got half a mind to lock him up
till I learn him some manners.

INT. ALAMO, GROUND-FLOOR OFFICE - DAY

The door opens and the two cops enter to find the window open, the screen torn and no sign of Godwin or the Device.

HINES
Better call the Rangers.

EXT. SAN ANTONIO ALLEY IN RESIDENTIAL NEIGHBORHOOD - DAY

Cuffs and sleeves rolled, belt cinched around his CHEST, Godwin clutches the Device as he picks his way in oversized PENNY LOAFERS down a deserted alley.

In the distance can be heard volleys of GUNFIRE, then a great ROAR and APPLAUSE. A band plays "THE EYES OF TEXAS."

Godwin PEERS through a CRACK in a fence.

EXT. BACK YARD - GODWIN'S P.O.V. - DAY

Near the gate is a pile of old newspapers and shopping bags.

Children's CLOTHES hang from clothes lines.

A PIE cools on a window sill.

EXT. BACK YARD - DAY

Godwin TIPTOES into the yard, DUCKING past the window.

A huge DOG bounds into the yard, GROWLING MENACINGLY.

Godwin GRABS the PIE and OFFERS it to the dog.

As the dog greedily attacks the pie, Godwin UNDRESSES.

EXT. SAN ANTONIO RESIDENTIAL STREET - DAY

Dressed in blue jeans, T-shirt and tennis shoes and carrying the Device and his adult clothes in a shopping bag, Godwin steps confidently down the quiet street.

INT. JIM BOWIE CAMERAS, DOWNTOWN SAN ANTONIO - DAY

Glass cases lined with new and used cameras and lenses. An elderly CLERK peers at a CATALOG as Godwin waits.

> CAMERA STORE CLERK
> What kind of camera was that?

> GODWIN
> Japanese. Thirty-five millimeter.

The clerk turns the catalog around and beckons to Godwin. He stands on TIPTOE to look.

                    CAMERA STORE CLERK
I'm pretty sure our Dallas store has one. Put it
on the morning Greyhound, I'll go get it after
lunch. 'Bout three o'clock?

                    GODWIN
Tomorrow?

                    CAMERA STORE CLERK
That a problem, son?

                    GODWIN
I was hoping to take some pictures before I go
home to...California.

EXT. STATE OFFICE BUILDING, DOWNTOWN SAN ANTONIO - DAY

To establish.

INT. OFFICE OF SAN ANTONIO COMMANDER, TEXAS RANGERS - DAY

A large office. Godwin's letters are spread over a big desk.

A TEXAS RANGERS MAJOR, 50s, tall, soup-strainer mustache, skin like
cowhide, regards Pugh and Hines with contempt.

                    MAJOR
And where is he now?

                    HINES
Uh, at large. Sir.

                    MAJOR
You two read these letters?

Both men nod.

                    MAJOR (CONT'D)
Wearing gloves, of course?

The pair inspect their boots, sheepish looks on their faces.

                    MAJOR (CONT'D)
After you two meet with the sketch artist, I want a list of
everyone who handled them. Everyone.

>   PUGH and HINES
>   Yes, sir.
>
>   MAJOR (CONT'D)
>   Boys--not a word about this to anyone, or I'll have your badges.

As they leave, the major picks up the phone.

>   MAJOR (CONT'D)
>   Get me Colonel Coulter in Dallas.

EXT. SAN ANTONIO PUBLIC LIBRARY - DAY

To establish.

INT. SAN ANTONIO PUBLIC LIBRARY - DAY

Clutching the shopping bag, Godwin prowls the stacks. He stops at a CLOSET, looks around, tries the door.

INT. LIBRARY CLOSET - DAY

Pitch black. Godwin flips the light switch and looks around: boxes of books, pamphlets. He turns the light OFF.

The door OPENS, revealing a WOMAN, 60s.

>   LIBRARIAN
>   Lost?
>
>   GODWIN
>   I thought it was the bathroom.

INT. LIBRARY - DAY

Godwin comes out of the bathroom. The librarian is WAITING.

>   LIBRARIAN
>   We closed at six. Next time you need a place to
>   stay until your parents get home -- young man,
>   do you know who John F. Kennedy is?
>
>   GODWIN
>   You mean the President?

OLD LIBRARIAN
He was in Berlin yesterday. That's in Germany.
He gave a speech there, and in a minute we're
going to watch it on TV. Will you join us?

INT. LIBRARY EMPLOYEE'S LOUNGE - DAY

Three old maid librarians sit on a couch while Godwin perches on a stool in
front of a small b/w television set.

On the TELEVISION SET, JFK addresses a huge throng in front of Berlin's City
Hall.

JFK
Two thousand years ago, the proudest boast in
the world was *"civis Romanus sum."*

GODWIN
(quietly) "I am a Roman citizen."

The librarians exchange GLANCES.

JFK
-in the world of freedom, the proudest boast is
"Ich bin ein Berliner."

The crowd CHEERS and applauds.

JFK (CONT'D)
... there are some who say that communism is
the wave of the future. *Let them come to Berlin.*
And there are some who say, in Europe and
elsewhere, we can work with the Communists.
*Let them come to Berlin! Lass' sie nach Berlin
kommen. Let them come to Berlin!*

Godwin SEES all three librarians dabbing at their eyes.

JFK (CONT'D)
-freedom has many difficulties and democracy is
not perfect, but we have never had to put a wall
up to keep our people in, to prevent them from
leaving us. All free men, wherever they may live,
are citizens of Berlin, and therefore, as a free
man, I take pride in the words, *"Ich bin ein
Berliner!"*

The crowd goes BONKERS.

Huge TEARS roll silently down Godwin's face.

He wipes his eyes. Face fixed with RESOLVE, Godwin grabs his shopping bag and leaves without a backward glance.

The librarians exchange perplexed looks.

INT. GREYHOUND BUS STATION, TICKET COUNTER - NIGHT

Godwin pushes cash under the window to a TICKET CLERK, 40s.

                    GODWIN
          One way to Dallas, please.

                    TICKET CLERK
          It's boarding now.

CLUTCHING his ticket, Godwin WHIRLS, COLLIDING with--

DEBBIE HORTON, 22, a petite, BIG-EYED, DARK-HAIRED beauty who bears a very strong resemblance to Godwin's late wife.

He is KNOCKED FLAT. The shopping bag BURSTS.

She HELPS him to his feet. Their eyes MEET. MAGIC.

                    DEBBIE
          You okay?

                    GODWIN
          (stammers) Nothing's broken...

A LONG AWKWARD SILENCE

                    DEBBIE
          You don't want to miss your bus...

Godwin gathers his stuff and, looking back over his shoulder at Debbie, RUNS toward the boarding area.

INT. GRAYHOUND BUS - NIGHT

Almost every seat is full.

Godwin sits on the aisle next to a dozing MEXICAN MAN, 40s.

The driver closes the doors with a pneumatic WHEEZE, SHIFTS into reverse, starts to back out.

SUDDENLY he brakes, shifts gears, moves forward, stops.

The doors open and TWO UNIFORMED COPS board.

They move down the aisle, LOOKING at every passenger. They stop at a row with a MEXICAN FAMILY: Husband, wife, 3 kids.

> FIRST COP
> Let's see some I.D., Pedro.

The man takes out his wallet and hands the cop a paper.

They move down the aisle and stop at Godwin's row.

Godwin PRETENDS to SLEEP.

> FIRST COP (CONT'D)
> Wake up! Lemme see some I.D.

Godwin opens ONE EYE.

> GODWIN
> (innocently) Uh, me?

> SECOND COP
> No, kid, Pedro. José. The Mex.

The first cop leans in and SHAKES the man awake.

> SECOND COP (CONT'D)
> Buenas nachos. Let's see some I.D.

Doing a SLOW BURN, the man produces a wallet. The cop GRABS it. He takes out a LICENSE and HANDS it to the First Cop.

> FIRST COP
> That's him.

> SECOND COP
> You're coming with us, Lopez.

> LOPEZ
> What for?

                    FIRST COP
Shut up. You can come easy, or we can have
ourselves a little fun.

                    GODWIN
What did he do?

                    FIRST COP
Police business, Sonny.

Lopez CLIMBS out and the cops escort him off the SILENT bus.

The driver REVS the engine, shifts into REVERSE, then stops.

The doors OPEN.

STRUGGLING with a suitcase, a woman boards. It's Debbie!

She comes down the aisle looking for an empty seat until she SEES Godwin.
She SMILES. He smiles back.

                    DEBBIE
          That seat taken?

Godwin shakes his head, no.

Debbie stows her bag and crawls over him to the window seat.

                    DEBBIE (CONT'D)
          I'm Debbie. What's your name?

                    GODWIN
Robert Godwin.

They shake hands, exchanging LOOKS.

                    DEBBIE
I'm so lucky! They said the bus was full. I was
already hating the idea of having to hang
around here till midnight. Then somebody got
off and now here *you* are again.

                    GODWIN
When I bumped into you before, I felt like you
looked right into my soul. As if we'd known each
other -- in a previous lifetime.

                              DEBBIE
          (laughs) You are soooo full of beans! What are
          you, 14, 15?

                              GODWIN
          Fate has brought us back together as soul
          mates. We must never be apart.

                              DEBBIE
          (LAUGHS) What a routine! Bet your daddy's a
          pistol!

She hands him a sandwich wrapped in waxed paper.

                         DEBBIE (CONT'D)
          Something tells me you like baloney.

Godwin unwraps the sandwich and begins to eat ravenously.

                              GODWIN
          (mouth full) Thanks.

The bus LURCHES into reverse and backs out of the terminal.

EXT. HIGHWAY 81, RURAL TEXAS - NIGHT

A Greyhound bus roars past a sign: Dallas: 68 miles.

INT. GREYHOUND BUS - NIGHT

Godwin and Debbie DOZE, his head pillowed on her shoulder. Sandwich
wrappers and crumbs litter their laps.

Debbie wakes up and starts to clean up, stuffing the trash in a paper bag.

Abruptly Godwin awakes. Momentarily confused by his circumstances and
surroundings, he looks around, NEAR PANIC.

                              DEBBIE
          It's all right, Bobby. Bad dream?

                              GODWIN
          For a minute I forgot where I was.

                    DEBBIE
Bobby, why are you traveling alone? What kind
of parents let a 16-year-old roam around Texas?

                    GODWIN
It's *Robert*. When I was a kid, I learned how to
take care of myself.

                    DEBBIE
When you were *a kid*?

                    GODWIN
I'm precocious. Anyway, school's out and I
wanted to watch the Alamo battle re-enactment
—it's only once a year. Dad had to work.

                    DEBBIE
What about your mom?

                    GODWIN
It's just me and Dad.

                    DEBBIE
I hate to be nosy, but why are you lugging
around such a big clock?

                    GODWIN
(snorts) My dad collects 'em. Before he let me go
to San Antonio I had promised to get it fixed.
But the repair guy was on vacation.

                    DEBBIE
Your Dad sounds like an interesting man. What
does he do?

                    GODWIN
Engineer. We just moved from Ohio.

                    DEBBIE
Well, you're gonna love Dallas. There's Little
League baseball, lots of swimming pools, the
Railroad Museum. You been to "Six Flags Over
Texas" yet?

                    GODWIN
I prefer the symphony.

                    DEBBIE
          Try to have some fun, Robert. You're only a kid
          once.

EXT. DALLAS GREYHOUND BUS TERMINAL ARRIVAL AREA - NIGHT

The San Antonio bus pulls in and people get off, among them Debbie and
Robert.

                    DEBBIE
          Very nice meeting you, Robert.

                    GODWIN
          The pleasure was mine.

                    DEBBIE
          My uncle's picking me up. Can we drop you
          somewhere?

                    GODWIN
          Dad said to call as soon as I got in. He'll come
          get me.

                    DEBBIE
          It's no trouble.

                    GODWIN
          Thanks anyway. And thanks for the sandwich.

Debbie opens her purse, pulls out a pad and scribbles. She RIPS the sheet out
and hands it to Robert.

                    DEBBIE
          If you need someone to show you around your
          new home town...

               A Chevy pickup pulls up and stops nearby.

                    DEBBIE (CONT'D)
          There's Uncle Ed. Bye!

She hurries off, struggling a little with the bag.

Godwin waits for the pickup to leave, then looks around. Across the street is a
NEON HOTEL LIGHT: VACANCY.

INT. HOTEL LAMAR - MIDNIGHT

Below desk level a clerk watches Johnny Carson on a b/w set.

                    GODWIN
          Excuse me...

The clerk looks up, sees nothing, returns to the TV.

                    GODWIN (CONT'D)
          Hello. Hello!

The clerk stands to peer OVER the counter and sees Godwin.

                    CLERK
          Ice at the end of the hall.

                    GODWIN
          I'd like a room.

                    CLERK
          Beat it. Go home and tell your old man you're
          sorry and you won't do it again.

                    GODWIN
          Excuse me! You know nothing of my personal
          life -- and it's none of your business anyway.
          (BEAT)
          I prefer not to make a scene, but your sign said
          "Vacancy" and I'm not leaving until you rent me
          a room.

The clerk gets to his feet and SIZES him up.

INT. DALLAS BUS TERMINAL - SUNRISE

Travelers wait on benches. In a darkened corner, under newspapers, Godwin
sleeps. Under the bench are candy wrappers and an empty Coke bottle. A
JANITOR guides a NOISY floor buffer across the tiles. As he approaches
Godwin stirs, sits up, yawning. He STRETCHES.

INT. DINER - DAY

At the counter Godwin reads the menu. A waitress appears.

                    WAITRESS
          What'll it be, honey?

                    GODWIN
          Cranberry juice. Scrambled egg whites. Rye
          toast, dry. Fruit instead of potatoes. One piece of
          bacon, very crisp.

The waitress regards Godwin skeptically.

                    WAITRESS
          This is Texas, sonny boy. The chicken serves a
          whole egg and so do we. You want juice, we got
          O.J. or tomato. White, wheat or biscuits with
          gravy. Grits, hash browns or home fries.

                    GODWIN
          The number one, please. Orange juice and a
          biscuit.

                    WAITRESS
          (to cook) Squeeze one, wreck two, side of
          Murphy, Cats heads and easy diggins, 86 the
          cow paste.

                    GODWIN
          Cup of Joe?

                    WAITRESS
          (shakes head, no) Moo juice for you.

As the waitress leaves, Godwin LOOKS AROUND at a diner full of well-worn
Stetsons and scuffed cowboy boots.

A MAN nearby STARES at him, all the while shoveling runny eggs, bloody
steak and grits into his weathered face.

EXT. ELM STREET, DALLAS - DAY

In brand new jeans and a T-shirt, Godwin steps off a city bus clutching an
OVERNIGHT BAG. He walks slowly down the street to the corner of Dealey
Plaza. Before him is a GRASSY KNOLL.

He looks around and spots a box-like, red-brick, six-story building: the TEXAS
BOOK DEPOSITORY.

Godwin weeps, wiping his eyes with the backs of his hands.

EXT. BEAUMONT STREET - NIGHT

Munching a burger, Godwin sits on a bus bench across from the Crawford Hotel, three sagging stories with barred windows.

He watches a young woman in a clinging, low-cut blouse walk arm-in-arm with a uniformed soldier. They enter the hotel.

After a BEAT a scantily-attired woman EXITS the Crawford.

A middle-aged man with a gal on each arm enters the hotel.

Godwin finishes his burger and dashes across the street.

INT. CRAWFORD HOTEL LOBBY - NIGHT

Worn chairs decorated with cigarette burns. A spittoon and a broken fan. Tattered curtains, stained linoleum. A dive.

A SHABBILY DRESSED MAN sits on the floor, pulling on boots.

Godwin approaches the **desk clerk**, SIGNALING WITH HIS EYES that he wants to talk. The clerk comes around the counter.

                    GODWIN
          How much for a room?

                    DESK CLERK
          Hit the road, punk.

Godwin holds up a $20 bill.

                    GODWIN
          Got a room for Mr. Jackson?

                    DESK CLERK
          No vacancies.

Godwin holds up a $50 bill.

                    GODWIN
          What about for Mr. Grant?

Smiling, he hands Godwin a key.

DESK CLERK
For another Grant, I could send someone up to
tuck you in?

GODWIN
I'm only a kid. Shouldn't I get tucked for half
price?

LAUGHING, the clerk WAGS a salacious finger at Godwin.

As Godwin waits for the elevator, the clerk EYES him, a PUZZLED LOOK on his
face: Something's not right.

INT. GODWIN'S ROOM IN CRAWFORD HOTEL - NIGHT

A bed, a scarred dresser, a night stand, sink, floor lamp.

Godwin SLEEPS on the lumpy bed.

The rhythmic sound of bed springs groaning under carnal coupling permeates
the room.

Down the hall a woman SHRIEKS.

A DOOR SLAMS.

CUSTOMER (O.C.)
You bitch! I had 40 bucks in this wallet when I
went to the bathroom.

WORKING WOMAN (O.C.)
So call the sheriff. And while you're at it, call
your wife.

Wearing PAJAMAS Godwin rolls off the bed, sleepy.

He opens the door, PEEKS OUT, leaves, shuts the door.

INT. HOTEL HALLWAY - NIGHT

Closing the bathroom door, Godwin heads back to his room.

He PASSES TWO HOOKERS, who glance at him CURIOUSLY.

He OPENS the door to his room.

INT. GODWIN'S HOTEL ROOM - NIGHT

Godwin ENTERS to SEE all the DRESSER DRAWERS are OPEN.

THE CONTENTS of his overnight bag are on the floor.

> GODWIN
> Hey! What are you doing in my room?

A SHABBILY DRESSED MAN holding the Device under his LEFT ARM TRIES to PUSH PAST HIM.

> SHABBILY DRESSED MAN
> Out of my way, half-pint!

Godwin RUSHES the man, HURLING HIMSELF at his belly.

The man staggers back. Godwin, on the floor, looks around.

The man gathers himself and heads for the open door.

Godwin grabs the floor lamp and SWEEPS it at the man's legs.

The BURGLAR TRIPS AND TUMBLES into the HALLWAY.

Godwin is on him in a fury, pounding him with small fists.

Doors open up and down the corridor and in moments they are surrounded by half-naked men and women in dishabille.

> GODWIN
> He stole my clock!

> SHABBILY DRESSED MAN
> What's a kid need with a fancy clock?

FLORA, 30s, high heels and loosely cinched kimono, KICKS the thief's head.

> FLORA
> What's a drunk need with teeth?

LUCILLE, 20s, very pretty, pulls Godwin off. Two JOHNS hoist the thief to his feet and pry the Device out of his grasp.

> LUCILLE
> You okay, kid?

The desk clerk clomps up the stairs, carrying a BASEBALL BAT.

                    DESK CLERK
          What the hell is going on?

                    LUCILLE
          Stuff it, Harry. Everybody knows you're all hat
          and no cattle.

The desk clerks SPOTS Godwin.

                    DESK CLERK
          I *knew* you were trouble, kid. You're outta here.

                    GODWIN
          But I paid...

                    DESK CLERK
          The kid ain't gone by daylight, all you girls are
          86 here for a month.

The desk clerk turns and walks away.

Godwin goes back into the room and starts to change clothes.

A knock on the door and after a beat Lucille enters.

                    LUCILLE
          You have some place to stay?

                    GODWIN
          Only my usual suite at the Hilton.

                    LUCILLE
          The streets around here aren't safe for a kid.

                    GODWIN
          I appreciate your concern.

                    LUCILLE
          Look, I'm done for the night. You want to crash
          on my couch?

Godwin pauses, thinking.

                    GODWIN
          How much?

                    LUCILLE
You think I let Johns spend the night with me
and my kid?

                    GODWIN
(ASHAMED) Sorry. I didn't...

                    LUCILLE
Get your things. My car's out back.

        AERIAL VIEW - DAYBREAK

Ringed by new housing tracts, four rows of aging trailers bake in the sun.
Mailboxes cluster at the entrance. MILK BOXES perch on stoops. Nearby: A
Piggly-Wiggly market.

CLOSER

A trailer with a corrugated iron roof and a TRICYCLE upended on a tiny patch
of dandelion-infested lawn.

INT. LUCILLE'S TRAILER - DAY

Covered with a sheet, Godwin snores softly on a couch.

AUSTIN, 5, toddles over to the couch and POKES Godwin. Again.

GODWIN'S P.O.V. - DAY

A chubby finger is POKING his face.

INT. LUCILLE'S TRAILER - DAY

Godwin sits up and stretches, SORE everywhere.

                    AUSTIN
        Time to eat!

                    GODWIN
You're hungry? Is that it?

                    AUSTIN
Hungry! Time to eat!

Godwin gets up, stretches, looks around.

Holding Austin's hand, he TAPS on the OPEN bedroom door.

INT. BEDROOM - DAY

Dirty clothes everywhere. A tiny dresser covered with every sort of makeup, perfume, lotion, skin cream, nail polish. Lucille sprawls on the bed, DEAD TO THE WORLD.

INT. TRAILER KITCHEN - DAY

A mess worse than the bedroom. Dirty glasses in the sink. Trash overflowing with paper plates and takeout cartons.

Godwin opens the refrigerator: Beer, a milk BOTTLE, a sprouting potato, greasy leftover chicken in a bucket.

Godwin SMELLS the milk. He WRINKLES his nose and empties the bottle into the sink. It comes out in a CLUMP.

                         AUSTIN
          Yucky!

Godwin LOOKS out the window and SEES the Piggly-Wiggly.

                         GODWIN
          C'mon, Let's go for a walk.

INT. LUCILLE'S KITCHEN, CLOSE ON STOVE - DAY

Steam rises from a PERFECT CHEESE and MUSHROOM OMELET.

COFFEE GURGLES in a percolator on the next BURNER.

INT. LUCILLE'S KITCHEN - CONTINUOUS

Standing on a MILK BOX to reach the stove top, Godwin deftly FOLDS and FLIPS the omelets. He steps down to open the broiler and SPEARS slices of toast, drops them in a WICKER BASKET lined with a PAPER TOWEL and puts it on the table.

He SLIDES the OMELETTE on a cluster of paper plates just as Lucille, bleary-eyed and unsteady, enters from the bedroom.

HAIR DOWN, NO MAKEUP, she SEEMS little more than a TEENAGER.

                    LUCILLE
          Something burning?

She SEES the repast on the tiny table. Austin eating toast.

                    LUCILLE (CONT'D)
          YOU did all this?

                    GODWIN
          Coffee?

                    LUCILLE
          We usually go out for breakfast...

                    GODWIN
          He was hungry...

She pours a cup of coffee, then sits down and LIGHTS UP.

                    GODWIN (CONT'D)
          You really shouldn't smoke around him. Second-
          hand smoke is bad for kids -- it may lead to
          asthma.

                    LUCILLE
          He's got a name -- Austin.

                    GODWIN
          Austin, my name is Robert.

                    LUCILLE
          And he don't like eggs.

                    GODWIN
          Lots of kids don't. That's why I added milk,
          cheese and mushrooms.

Austin holds up his EMPTY plate for more.

                    AUSTIN
          Yummy eggs, Lucy!

OFF A LOOK BY GODWIN

Lucille takes a last puff, exhales AWAY from Austin, puts out the cigarette and
FANS the air.

EXT. OLD RED COURTHOUSE, DALLAS - DAY

A turreted Victorian monstrosity faced in red sandstone.

INT. COURTHOUSE CORRIDOR, TEXAS RANGERS REGIONAL OFFICE - DAY

In step, two TEXAS RANGERS in business suits march down the corridor and through a door marked "Commanding Officer."

INT. COLONEL COULTER'S OFFICE - DAY

The Rangers STAND facing a massive oak desk. Behind the desk is COL. EDWIN COULTER, 50s, tall, beefy, gray buzz-cut, ruddy complexion, gut hanging over a fancy belt buckle. His SNAKE SKIN COWBOY BOOTS rest on the desk, their fancy VAMPS adorned with the HEAD and EXPOSED FANGS of a rattler.

>   COL. COULTER
>   Well?

RANGER FICKE, 35, balding, ten pounds of pork in a nine-pound bag, glances at his notes.

>   FICKE
>   Oswald's no Boy Scout.
>   Faked a hardship discharge from the Marines.
>   Lived in Russia for years.
>
>   Speaks Russian -- even married a Ruskie bitch.
>   FBI carries an open file on them. Both down in
>   New Orleans now. He's working, seems to be
>   keeping his nose clean.
>
>   They're expecting a second baby.

>   COL. COULTER
>   What about the Beckley boarding house? He ever
>   stay there?

>   FICKE
>   They never heard of him there, sir.

>   COL. COULTER
>   Who called the White House?

RANGER LUNDGREN, 30s, taller, pulls out a pad.

                    LUNDGREN
Secret Service gets a *lot* of mail. Mostly lunatic
fringe crap. They say the President's not
scheduled to return to Texas this year.

                    COL. COULTER
Scheduled. Huh. Let me know if that changes.
Now, what about that kid?

Ficke looks up.

                    FICKE
He came up on the Greyhound. Walked around
Elm Street, bought clothes and a bag. About
dark yesterday he went into the Crawford Hotel.

                    COL. COULTER
That whorehouse on Beaumont?

Ficke nods, yes.

                    COL. COULTER (CONT'D)
We have someone in there?

                    LUNDGREN
Yessir.

                    COL. COULTER
Who wrote the letters?

                    LUNDGREN
Not that kid. His prints are on 'em, but
linguistic analysis indicates the author is a
college graduate, an accomplished writer.

                    COL. COULTER
Huh.

                    LUNDGREN
Those letters got the Crime Lab boys scratching
their pointy little heads. The paper seems to
have been made from ground-up old
newspapers.

Re-manufactured stuff. Definitely *not* made in
the USA.

COL. COULTER

Then where?

LUNDGREN

Russia, maybe. China. Shoot, Outer Mongolia!
Next, the ink. They've never seen nothing like it.
Can't even figure how it was applied to the
paper.

Their best guess is that it was printed by some
high-level spook outfit. NSA or CIA, maybe.

COL. COULTER

KGB? GRU?

LUNDGREN

Could be. Finally there's the addressing. You
know this new ZIP-code thing? Starts next
month?

COL. COULTER

Damn post office clowns. What a pain in the ass
that's gonna be!

LUNDGREN

Well, it's a five-number deal. Optional, for now.
But every one of the letter addresses was NINE
numbers. The ZIP, plus four more.

COL. COULTER

Meaning?

LUNDGREN

Postmaster General's office just about went loco
when I called. "Zip Plus Four" is classified --
even the program *title* is secret -- and I'm not
need-to-know. Can you believe those guys?

FICKE

So the guy who wrote these letters--

COL. COULTER

-- has access to top-secret Federal information.
Huh. *Huh.*

                    FICKE
Let's grab the kid -- shake him up, scare him
shitless.

                    COL. COULTER
Then we might could lose the letter-writer. And
anybody else... But if Kennedy ain't coming back
to Texas, he ain't *my* problem. For now, just
keep an eye on the kid. See where he leads us.

EXT. PUBLIC SWIMMING POOL, DALLAS - DAY

A big pool busy with ALL-WHITE lifeguards, kids and moms. A SIGN near the
entrance reads: WHITE ONLY.

Godwin sits next to Austin in the SHALLOWS. Wearing a modest one-piece suit,
Lucille dangles her feet in the water.

                    GODWIN
Austin, let's blow some bubbles.

                    AUSTIN
Blow bubbles!

                    LUCILLE
You sure you know what you're doing?

                    GODWIN
Absolutely. All kids are natural swimmers --
after all, they spent nine months floating in a
womb.

                    LUCILLE
I never looked at it like that.

Godwin HOLDS HIS BREATH, puts his mouth and nose under the water, blows
bubbles, then lifts his head.

                    GODWIN
(to Austin) Just like that.

Austin holds his breath, blows bubbles. He emerges laughing.

                    GODWIN (CONT'D)
Watch me, Austin.

Godwin reclines, relaxes, and allows himself to FLOAT.

Austin floats alongside until Godwin STANDS. Austin does too.

                    GODWIN (CONT'D)
          Now let's float on our bellies.

                    LUCILLE
          I don't know about this...

OFF a LOOK from Godwin.

Godwin and Austin float face down. After a beat, both stand.

                    GODWIN
          Now let's splash.

EXT. PUBLIC SWIMMING POOL, DALLAS - LATER

               Lucille and Godwin soak their feet in the
               shallow end, watching as Austin SWIMS happily
               nearby.

                    AUSTIN
          Lucy! I swimmed the whole way!

                    LUCILLE
          You're a natural-born teacher, Bobby.

                    GODWIN
          So I've been told.

                    LUCILLE
          Travis kept promising to teach him, but he
          never got around to it.

                    GODWIN
          Travis -- your boyfriend?

                    LUCILLE
          More like my... business manager.

                    GODWIN
          Your pimp?

                    LUCILLE
          Young man, you got mouth enough for an
          alligator farm! Watch it, hear?

                    GODWIN
Sorry.

                    LUCILLE
Bobby, where are your folks? If you don't mind
me asking...

                    GODWIN
They died when I was little. I was in foster care,
then a sort of orphanage. Like a prison for kids.

                    LUCILLE
I knew it--you're a runaway!

                    GODWIN
Takes one to know one?

Lucille LAUGHS.

                    LUCILLE
I fooled around and got pregnant when I was
15. After that my step-daddy thought he could
do anything he wanted to me, and when I said
"no," he whupped me.

                    GODWIN
Why didn't you tell your mom?

                    LUCILLE
She said I was a tramp and it was my fault that
he... Then she tried to take me to some doctor in
Juarez... Anyway, I just took off.

Austin splashes by.

                    AUSTIN
Watch this, Bobby!

                    LUCILLE
Austin really likes you.

                    GODWIN
He's a great little kid. Who watches him when
you're, uh....

                    LUCILLE
You ever baby sit?

                    GODWIN
Sure.

                    LUCILLE
Want to stay with us for a while?
Watch Austin while I'm working?

                    GODWIN
For *awhile*. Thanks, Lucy.

                    LUCILLE
And Bobby, could you show me how to make
that omelets? And the toast?

INT. LUCILLE'S TRAILER - DAY

The kitchen is spic and span. Godwin dries dishes.

Lucille appears, all tarted up in a SLINKY, REVEALING DRESS. She coughs
until he LOOKS, then SPINS theatrically.

                    LUCILLE
Ta-da! What do you think?

                    GODWIN
(Insincere) Very flattering.

                    LUCILLE
If you want to catch big fish, you gotta use the
good bait!

                    GODWIN
(uncomfortable) I guess.

                    LUCILLE
(Hurt) You don't like it.

                    GODWIN
I just think you're... better than that.

                    LUCILLE
So you don't like what I do!

                    GODWIN
Do you?

                    LUCILLE
          Don't you think I'd rather be a secretary? Or a
          bookkeeper? But I never even finished high
          school and now I've got a kid to raise!

                    GODWIN
          Trust me -- everybody has choices. Usually, the
          long way around is the short way home...

Pondering, Lucy takes out a cigarette and LIGHTS UP.

Godwin COUGHS and LOOKS over at Austin, coloring in a book.

Lucy rolls her eyes and STUBS out the cigarette.

                    GODWIN (CONT'D)
          Lucy, do you know where I can borrow a
          typewriter?

                    LUCILLE
          Don't tell me you *type,* too?

                    GODWIN
          A little.

                    LUCILLE
          Sometimes you scare me. You cook. You know
          to fix things. Half the time you use words I
          never heard -- and Austin's crazy about you.
          Who are you. I mean, for real?

                    GODWIN
          (robot's voice) I. Am. A. Time. Traveler. From.
          The. 21st Century. I. Come. To. Save. The.
          World. From. A. Great. Tragedy.

Austin is DELIGHTED and ENCHANTED with the robot voice.

                    AUSTIN
          More! Talk more, Bobby!

                    GODWIN
          (robot voice) But. First. I. Need. A. Typewriter.
          (Tickles Austin) AND. YOU. MUST. GO. TO. BED.

Austin GIGGLES.

                              LUCILLE
            You gotta be the weirdest kid I ever met. Try the
            public library, Bobby. Ten cents an hour.

EXT. TIMBER GLENN BRANCH, DALLAS PUBLIC LIBRARY - DAY

An aging two-story stone building.

INT. TYPING ROOM, TIMBER GLENN BRANCH, DALLAS PUBLIC LIBRARY

Four desks with coin-operated Olympia typewriters.

Godwin sits between two women typing.

Godwin slips a fresh page in and types FURIOUSLY until the women on either
side of him look up, quizzically.

Self-conscious, he SWITCHES to HUNT and PECK.

INT. LIBRARY BOOK CHECKOUT DESK - DAY

MISS POOLE, YOUNG and PLAIN, looks at his books: "Horton Hears A Who," a
Dr. Seuss book, "Basic Accounting," and "To Kill A Mockingbird" by Harper Lee.

                         MISS POOLE
                              For your mom?

                         GODWIN
                              And my little
                              brother.

                         MISS POOLE
            Nothing for you?

Godwin holds up a pair of addressed envelopes.

                         GODWIN
            Where can I get stamps?

                         MISS POOLE
            Drugstore, down the street. It's five cents now!
            Highway robbery!

INT. CORNER DRUGSTORE - DAY

Licking an ice cream cone, Godwin places a tiny CAMERA BATTERY on the counter.

                    GODWIN
          You sell stamps?

The counter clerk indicates a stamp vending MACHINE next to a COMMUNITY BULLETIN BOARD with NOTICES on 3 x 5 CARDS.

EXT. CORNER DRUGSTORE - DAY

Carrying the books and licking the cone, Godwin exits, walks to a MAIL BOX and deposits two envelopes.

EXT. LIBERTY JUNIOR HIGH SCHOOLYARD, DALLAS - DAY

Eating the last of the ice cream, Godwin walks along the sidewalk and stops to watch a bunch of BOYS playing baseball.

The batter hits a ground ball to the shortstop, who bobbles it and throws LATE to first.

A new batter. The pitcher throws the ball. The batter swings.

A ball arcs high toward JOEY, an outfielder. He misjudges it and the ball bounces past and rolls through to the sidewalk.

                    JOEY
          Hey! A little help!

Godwin puts his books down, picks up the ball and pegs a strong throw back to the infield.

                    JOEY (CONT'D)
          Wanna play?

Godwin gathers his books.

                    GODWIN
          Gotta baby-sit.

INT. TEXAS RANGERS, COL. COULTER'S OFFICE - DAY

FICKE places a LETTER in a plastic cover on Coulter's desk.

                    FICKE
Governor's office got this Friday. Kid's prints are
all over it.

                    COL. COULTER
And the kid is where?

                    FICKE
I'd say pretty close to where this was
postmarked -- Timber Glenn.

                    COL. COULTER
So we've lost him. And the typewriter?

                    FICKE
Olympia Standard, Model SG. Only about 2,000
in Texas. Maybe half in the public libraries.

                    COL. COULTER
Why are you still here?

Ficke waddles from the room.

INT. LUCILLE'S TRAILER - DAY

Coffee perks on the stove as Godwin reaches into a well-stocked refrigerator
and comes out with a carton of eggs and a bottle of orange juice as Lucy enters
from the bedroom.

                    GODWIN
          Breakfast?

He SEES that Lucy has a BLACK EYE and a SPLIT LIP.

                    GODWIN (CONT'D)
What happened to you?

                    LUCILLE
Bobby, we need to talk.

                    GODWIN
Travis did that?

                    LUCILLE
There was some kind of cop at the hotel. At the
Crawford. He had a picture of you. Like a
cartoon.

GODWIN
A sketch? You're sure it was me?

LUCILLE
A boy with a clock. It was you.

GODWIN
Shit!

LUCILLE
Watch your mouth! Bobby, this cop -- he wasn't
like the ones who come in to pick up the
envelope every week. He had a nice suit. I think
he might be FBI.

GODWIN
Why would the FBI want me?

LUCILLE
I was hoping *you'd* tell *me.*

GODWIN
This FBI guy -- *he* hit you?

LUCILLE
Uh-uh. Just asked if I'd seen you.
Flora told him that we were talking that night. I
said that I just dropped you off at the
Greyhound.

GODWIN
Then who did that to you?

LUCILLE
This cop gave me $50. Said there was more if I
helped find you. Travis musta heard-- this
morning he said I held out on him for his half of
the fifty.

GODWIN
Let me put some ice on your eye.

LUCILLE
Bobby, what did you do?

GODWIN
I told you. I ran off.

                    LUCILLE
No way the FBI's spreading money around for a
runaway. Bobby, talk to me. Maybe I can help.

                    GODWIN
I... I... I can't.

                    LUCILLE
Nothing you could say would shock me. I've
heard it all.

                    GODWIN
I've caused you enough trouble. I'll get my
things.

                    LUCILLE
And go where?

                    GODWIN
I'll figure it out.

                    LUCILLE
Bobby, what did you do? Please.

                    GODWIN
Lucy, listen to me. I was never in an orphanage.
I lived with my uncle in Dayton, Ohio. My folks
died when I was seven and left me a lot of
money. A trust fund. I get a monthly allowance,
but when I'm 21 I get it all: About $3 million.

                    LUCILLE
Good lord!

                    GODWIN
But if I die before I'm 21, my uncle gets the
money. He tried to kill me, so I ran away.

Lucy eyes him skeptically.

                    LUCILLE
You blow more wind than a corn-eating plow
horse!

                    GODWIN
It's the truth.

                    LUCILLE
You got *some* imagination.

                    GODWIN
You said you wanted to help?

                    LUCILLE
But if Travis finds out...

                    GODWIN
I won't put you and Austin in danger. If I give
you some money, could you rent me a place to
stay?

                    LUCILLE
And then what?

                    GODWIN
I've got something to take care of here. In a few
months, I'll go back to Ohio and find a judge I
know. He was my father's friend, but he's out of
the country for awhile.

                    LUCILLE
You sure pile it high and deep! But you're a kid.
You can't look out for yourself. Not yet.

                    GODWIN
You trust me to take care of Austin. Why can't
you trust me to take care of myself?

EXT. TIMBER GLENN BRANCH, DALLAS PUBLIC LIBRARY - MORNING.

A '57 Chevy stops in front of the building.

INT. '57 CHEVY - DAY

Godwin turns to the driver: Lucille.

                    LUCILLE
Why can't you just come with me?

                    GODWIN
What if they're watching you? Better we say
goodbye now. Remember what I said about the
drug store?

                    LUCILLE
You wrote it down for me, Bobby.

                    GODWIN
The key?

                    LUCILLE
Wrote that down, too. Like *I'm* the kid. (ROLLS
EYES) The apartment will have to be in my
name, so if anyone asks, you're my kid brother,
Bobby Schmidlap.

                    GODWIN
Schmidlap? Really?

                    LUCILLE
Like Mom always says, would a real Texan make
up a name like that?

                    GODWIN
Actually, it's German. Like the 16th century
rocket scientist, Johann Schmidlap.

                    LUCILLE
You are one strange boy, Bobby.

                    GODWIN
Rent the apartment. Then forget about me.

                    LUCILLE
You sure you're gonna be okay?

They embrace. Lucille STIFLES a SOB.

                    GODWIN
One more thing.

He gives her a BULGING envelope.

Lucille OPENS it. Her eyes go WIDE.

                    GODWIN (CONT'D)
If you're careful, that should be enough for a
couple of years.

                    LUCILLE
I couldn't...

                    GODWIN
          Just take some clothes and Austin. Leave
          everything else. Go to Chicago, Denver, L.A. Lose
          yourself. Get your high school diploma, find a
          job. Start over.

                    LUCILLE
          How much did you steal, Bobby?

                    GODWIN
          I'm *not* a thief. Now go. Rent me a place, get out
          of Texas. Today!

Lucille bursts into tears as Godwin jumps out. Lugging a HEAVY overnight bag
and some books, he runs into the library.

EXT. LUCILLE'S TRAILER - DAY

Now empty-handed, Godwin retrieves a KEY from a flower pot. He glances
CURIOUSLY at a shiny, new, '63 red-and-white CADILLAC CONVERTIBLE
parked nearby.

INT. LUCILLE'S TRAILER - DAY

Godwin pushes open the door, grabs a second overnight bag--

-- and is JERKED off his feet by TRAVIS, 30s, six feet, four inches of muscular
menace and dark hair thick with POMADE.

                    TRAVIS
               I knew it!

Travis holds Godwin, SQUIRMING and KICKING, at arm's length and SQUINTS
at a drawing of Godwin's face -- a good likeness.

                    GODWIN
               Let me down, you cretin!

Not sure if he's been insulted, Travis SLAPS Godwin anyway.

                    TRAVIS
          What'd you do? Rape somebody's baby sister?
          Little pervert!

Travis SLAPS him again for good measure.

EXT. LUCILLE'S TRAILER - DAY

Holding Godwin under one arm, Travis awkwardly opens the door of the CADDY. Godwin grabs a finger and BITES.

> TRAVIS
> Sonofabitch!

Travis DROPS Godwin.

Godwin scrambles to his feet but Travis grabs him, slaps his face, hard. He falls, his nose BLEEDING.

> TRAVIS (CONT'D)
> That reward ain't big enough, I'm gonna beat
> you bloody and turn you out for the fag trade.

Holding Godwin by his collar, Travis opens the trunk, tosses the overnight bag in, then Godwin. He slams the trunk closed.

Travis looks at his finger. It's bleeding. He drives off.

EXT. BEAUMONT STREET - DAY

The Caddy stops across from the Crawford Hotel and Travis gets out. He walks to the rear and POUNDS it hard. He bends to put his head next to the trunk.

> TRAVIS
> I'm gonna open up now. Try anything and I'll
> just cold-cock ya.

Travis opens the trunk.

He bends forward to grab Godwin, who

SLAMS a LUG WRENCH into his FACE with all his might.

Travis STAGGERS backward as --

Godwin SCRATCHES a SAFETY FLARE against the trunk lid.

With a BELLOW of RAGE, Travis LEAPS at Godwin, who

SHOVES the RED FLAME into his face.

Travis SCREAMS as his pomaded HAIR bursts into FLAME.

As Travis frantically beats his head, Godwin grabs his bag and jumps down to the street.

He turns, tosses the flare into the trunk and RUNS.

He's halfway down the block when the CADDY EXPLODES.

EXT. CORNER DRUGSTORE NEAR TIMBER GLENN LIBRARY - TWILIGHT

Carrying the bag, Godwin gets off a bus and, after looking around carefully, enters the drugstore.

INT. CORNER DRUGSTORE - TWILIGHT

Godwin peers at the bulletin board. He REMOVES a hand-printed card. The card reads:

ROOM FOR RENT

13224 McBride Ave., #202

John Le Carré

555-7609

Godwin pockets the card and strolls to the ice cream counter.

EXT. HUNTER APARTMENTS - NIGHT

Three floors of weathered brick and wrought-iron fire escapes. Dragging the bag, Godwin trudges up the walk. He checks the card, peers at the address: 2231.

INT. HUNTER APARTMENTS - NIGHT

Godwin moves down a dim hallway. The muted voice of JOHNNY CASH's "RING OF FIRE" oozes through a door. He stops in front of *203*, where the THEME from BONANZA booms from a TV within.

Cautiously, he lifts the welcome mat to find a KEY.

INT. APARTMENT 202 - NIGHT

Godwin enters, finds a light switch and looks around. A chair, a bed, a table, a tiny kitchen. A shopping bag sits on the bed, and he peers inside: New bed sheets and a pillow.

He opens the fridge: A wrapped sandwich. A carton of MILK.

He pulls down the window shade, kicks off his shoes and collapses on the unmade bed, utterly spent.

EXT. TIMBER GLENN BRANCH, DALLAS PUBLIC LIBRARY - DAY

A brown 1962 Ford Fairlane is parked in a NO-PARKING zone.

INT. TIMBER GLENN BRANCH, DALLAS PUBLIC LIBRARY - DAY

Ranger Ficke inspects the typewriters, noting their models.

INT. TIMBER GLENN BRANCH LIBRARY, INFORMATION DESK - DAY

Ficke shows Miss Poole a PENCIL SKETCH of Godwin.

                    FICKE
          You ever see this kid?

                    MISS POOLE
          Who wants to know?

Ficke holds up a BADGE.

                    FICKE
          The people of Texas.

                    MISS POOLE
          He's a very nice young man.

                    FICKE
          He ever come in with someone?

                    MISS POOLE
          He's always alone. What'd he do?

                    FICKE
          It's a police matter. When's the last time you saw
          this boy?

                    MISS POOLE
A few weeks ago. Checked out some books, used
a typewriter.

                    FICKE
What books?

                    MISS POOLE
I'm afraid *that* is no business of the State of
Texas.

                    FICKE
Look missy -- we have every right to know what
he's been reading.

                    MISS POOLE
You'll find the U.S. Constitution under 353.1 in
Government and History. I suggest you read it.

After a long BEAT, Ficke turns on his heel and leaves.

INT. GODWIN'S APARTMENT - DAY

Puffing on a CIGAR and clutching a CRAYON, Godwin PACES in front of a big
sheet of WHITE BUTCHER PAPER taped to a wall.

At the top of the paper its says:

          Nov. 22, noon? **JFK shot.**
          Nov. 21? **LHO gets gun from Irving Garage?**
          Nov. 20? Times Herald prints motorcade route

          Oct. ? Marina goes to Paine home, LHO puts gun garage.

          Oct. 16? Oswald starts work at School Book Depository.

          Oct. 14? LHO rents Beckley room.

          Oct. 3? LHO arrives Dallas?

          Sept.?   JFK trip to Dallas announced.

Godwin picks up a RED crayon and CIRCLES "gun and garage."

He continues puffing and pacing, thinking furiously.

INT. TIMBER GLENN BRANCH, DALLAS PUBLIC LIBRARY - DAY

Deep in the GLOOM of the STACKS, Godwin sits cross-legged and peers at a PICTURE BOOK with EXPLODED VIEWS of GUNS.

He TRACES a MAUSER action, then hides the book near a dusty volume of Thucydides "History of the Peloponnesian War."

Leaving, he passes Miss Poole. He notices her STARING at him.

EXT. TIMBER GLENN BRANCH, DALLAS PUBLIC LIBRARY - DAY

Godwin pauses on the front steps and looks around. He SEES the BROWN FAIRLANE parked next to a NO PARKING sign.

Godwin hesitates, then turns and hurries back inside.

EXT. TIMBER GLENN BRANCH PUBLIC LIBRARY REAR ENTRANCE - DAY

The door OPENS and Godwin SLIPS out.

INT. DALLAS CITY BUS - DAY

Rear rows are occupied exclusively by black people. Seated among whites on the half-full bus, Godwin reads the sports page. A headline announces: "COLT .45s FIRE BLANKS." A big AD on the back page touts a Fourth Of July Sale.

EXT. DALLAS STREET - DAY

Several cars behind the bus, the brown Fairlane follows.

EXT. BRASS RAIL GUNS - DAY

A big store selling all manner of sporting firearms and ammo.

INT. BRASS RAIL GUNS - DAY

Godwin waits quietly at a counter backed by RIFLE RACKS as a SALESMAN, 40s, sells ammo to a man. As the man leaves with his purchase, the salesman looks at Godwin.

                    GUN SALESMAN
          Howdy, boy! Whatcha need today? Some .22 long
          rifle? Targets?

                    GODWIN
Uh, no. Mister, my dad says I could get a rifle
for my birthday.

                    GUN SALESMAN
You come to the right place.

                    GODWIN
But my mom says I'm too young. She thinks it's
dangerous...

                    GUN SALESMAN
(SNORTS) Women.

                    GODWIN
Anyway, she said that if I wrote a summer-
school paper that shows I know how a rifle
works, she'd maybe change her mind.

                    GUN SALESMAN
So you'd like to see a rifle?

                    GODWIN
And could you maybe take one apart and show
me how it works and everything?

                    GUN SALESMAN
Where's your dad?

                    GODWIN
He works for Texas Instruments. He's out in
California this week.

The salesman turns, selects a rifle from the rack and places it on the counter
in front of Godwin.

                    GUN SALESMAN
This is an Enfield .303. It's a little big for you
now, but it's pretty much like all bolt-actions.

                    GODWIN
Does it have a Mauser action?

                    GUN SALESMAN
Just about the same, yeah.

                    GODWIN
          How does the bullet get fired?

The salesman turns the rifle on its side, LEVERS the bolt open and points to a
small HOLE in the face of the BOLT.

                    GUN SALESMAN
          See that hole? Pull the trigger and the hammer
          strikes the firing pin. It comes through the hole
          and hits the back of the cartridge. Bang.

                    GODWIN
          What if the pin is too long?

                    GUN SALESMAN
          Never seen that. Only way would be if you had
          the wrong pin. Then when you close the bolt on
          a round, it'd fire without the trigger. Very
          dangerous.

                    GODWIN
          But what if it was too short? The firing pin?

                    GUN SALESMAN
          You sure ask a lot of questions! Well, sometimes
          that pin wears down. Then it can't make contact
          with the cartridge. Won't fire.

          See, that's what they do with the rifles those
          boys use over in the high school ROTC. They
          take a file to the firing pin, shorten it a touch,
          then it's safe.

                    GODWIN
          Could you show me how to take the bolt apart?

SIGHING, the salesman begins to disassemble the rifle.

EXT. BRASS RAIL GUNS - DAY

As Godwin leaves the store, he NOTICES the brown Fairlane parked next to a
HYDRANT.

He strolls to the corner bus stop, PRETENDING to window shop.

A bus stops at the corner. Passengers get off. Some get on.

As the light CHANGES the bus driver closes the door.

As the bus pulls away, Godwin DASHES for its rear and LEAPS onto the bumper, CLINGING to the rear window grill.

Amazingly fast for a man his size, Ficke DASHES to his car.

EXT. REAR OF BUS - DAY

Godwin LOOKS back over his shoulder and SEES the Fairlane run the red light behind him. As the bus SLOWS for traffic, Godwin LEAPS down and DARTS into the street.

He DODGES honking cars and trucks to cross the street.

FICKE STOPS his car, JUMPS out and runs after Godwin, waving a BADGE as he hustles into traffic.

As Godwin makes the other side he SEES a BACKHOE excavating the street. A pile of big corrugated steel PIPE is stacked nearby. Ficke on his heels, Godwin JUMPS into the hole.

Ficke SEES Godwin disappears into a two-foot round conduit.

INT. UNDERGROUND ELECTRICAL CONDUIT - DAY

Godwin CRAWLS on hands and knees toward a SHAFT of LIGHT.

EXT. DALLAS ALLEY - DAY

Godwin emerges from an open MANHOLE just as FICKE appears at the mouth of the alley.

Godwin LOOKS AROUND and takes off up a short but STEEP slope.

As he tops the hill a DELIVERY TRUCK turns into the street.

Running hard, he overtakes the slow-moving truck. He leaps and pulls himself onto the tailgate.

He looks back at FICKE and WAVES "BYE-BYE," TAUNTING him.

The truck STOPS in front of a store. Ficke picks up the pace as Godwin scrambles down and runs into a HARDWARE store.

INT. HARDWARE STORE - DAY

Godwin dashes through, scattering bins of nuts, bolts, screws, light bulbs, nails, etc., etc., behind him as obstacles to Ficke. Customers tumble like bowling pins.

EXT. REAR ENTRANCE HARDWARE STORE - DAY

Godwin comes flying out the building past kids cooling themselves in spray from a hydrant. As Ficke appears. Godwin dashes across the street and into a four-story building.

INT. FOUR STORY BUILDING - DAY

Godwin pushes the elevator buttons and SEES it's 3 floors up. He runs to the stairs just as Ficke bursts into the building.

INT. FOUR STORY BUILDING STAIRWELL - DAY

Tiring, Godwin reaches the fourth floor and pauses to LISTEN. Hearing nothing, he leans against a wall, PANTING.

Suddenly the elevator DINGS. Its doors OPEN, revealing Ficke.

                    FICKE
          Gotcha!

Godwin ducks away and turns into a side corridor.

He finds a ladder to the roof and starts climbing.

EXT. FOUR STORY BUILDING ROOF - DAY

Godwin emerges from the TRAP DOOR onto the tar-covered roof.

He moves to the edge, feet STICKING to the soft tar. He looks down: the next roof is ten feet away and 15 feet below.

He looks at the trap door just as Ficke SQUEEZES his bulky frame through the NARROW opening, RIPPING his suit.

                    FICKE
          Your skinny ass is mine!

Savoring the moment, Ficke approaches, DANGLING HANDCUFFS.

Godwin looks around. He jumps UP on a low brick wall ringing the roof.

He LEAPS.

EXT. ADJACENT ROOF - DAY

Godwin lands on a shoulder and ROLLS.

Above him, FICKE TEETERS on the rooftop wall.

FICKE'S P.O.V. - DAY

He looks at the roof. At the alley below. At Godwin.

EXT. ADJACENT ROOF - DAY

FICKE comes hurtling up and over, FEET FIRST.

He CRASHES THROUGH THE WARM, SOFT, TAR-PAPER ROOF and buries himself up to his massive chest.

Godwin gets up and walks to an open stairwell. He HESITATES, then turns back to APPROACH Ficke.

>   GODWIN
>   Why are you chasing *me*?

>   FICKE
>   Who wrote those letters?

>   GODWIN
>   Lee Harvey Oswald wants to kill President
>   Kennedy. Stop him.

>   FICKE
>   Who do you work for? Who sent you?

>   GODWIN
>   Tell the President that he must *not* come to
>   Dallas this November.

>   FICKE
>   You can't run forever.

                    GODWIN
I'm only trying to help.

                    FICKE
(moans) I think my ankle's broken.

                    GODWIN
I'll call 911.

                    FICKE
Huh?

Godwin walks to the stairs, pauses, then turns around again.

                    GODWIN
And you really ought to do something about
your weight...

INT. COL. COULTER'S OFFICE - DAY

Ficke, ON CRUTCHES, and Lundgren face Col. Coulter's desk.

                    FICKE
First time I broke that ankle was in '48, at the
Cotton Bowl, when we creamed Penn State.

                    LUNDGREN
What'd you do, fall off the bench?

Ficke looks WOUNDED.

                    COL. COULTER
Boys. Got a telex this morning from the
governor's office. New plan: The President
arrives November 22. We *need* to find that kid.

                    LUNDGREN
Every sighting we have, plus the postmarks, put
him within two miles of the TIMBER GLENN
branch library.

                    COL. COULTER
If there's a plot to kill Kennedy, we can be damn
sure this Oswald's got nothing to do with it.
(BEAT)
Whoever's running this game on us knows way

too much to be anything but a Fed. So, not a
peep to our Fibbie pals. I mean it!

EXT. TRAILER PARK - DAY

A battered PINK-AND-WHITE 1955 Ford Convertible stops in front of Lucille's
trailer and Travis gets out.

His STETSON fails to conceal the BANDAGE covering his pate. Both eyes show
recent shiners; his nose is bandaged.

He looks around furtively. He goes to the flower pot. Empty.

He knocks on the door. A blowsy, middle-aged blonde in a housecoat answers.

                    WOMAN
          What happened to you, handsome?

                    TRAVIS
          You should see the other guy.

She peers at his parked car.

                    WOMAN
          Something tells me you ain't the Fuller Brush
          man.

                    TRAVIS
          Lucy around?

                    WOMAN
          Nobody here but us chickens.

                    TRAVIS
          I'm looking for a blonde, a baby, and a 12-year-
          old kid named Bobby.

                    WOMAN
          Well, *I'm* a blonde.

                    TRAVIS
          Hers don't come out of a bottle.

                    WOMAN
          (miffed) Well, she moved.

                              TRAVIS
                    Any idea where she went?

                              WOMAN
                    Nope. But now I see why they was in such a
                    hurry to leave that they left half their stuff.

The woman SLAMS the DOOR shut.

INT. GODWIN'S APARTMENT - NIGHT

The shade is DOWN. CONSULTING a MAGAZINE, Godwin uses one of several
X-Acto KNIVES to carve BALSA wood into the ORNATE PROW of a three-foot-
long ANCIENT GREEK SAILING SHIP.

INT. GODWIN'S APARTMENT - DAY

PAPERBACK books are STACKED near the bed. Every flat surface is covered
with a PLASTIC MODEL -- a YANKEE CLIPPER SHIP, a V-8 ENGINE, A WORLD
WAR II BOMBER.

Godwin drinks coffee and watches "Queen For A Day."

INT. GODWIN'S APARTMENT - NIGHT

"Ben Casey" plays on TV while Godwin does sit-ups. He switches to push-ups.

INT. GODWIN'S APARTMENT - DAY

Godwin READS "Crime and Punishment" while a tinny transistor radio plays
"Easier Said Than Done," by The Essex.

Abruptly he turns off the radio and STRETCHES.

EXT. LIBERTY JUNIOR HIGH SCHOOLYARD - DAY

Kids play baseball. JOEY, a husky, dark-haired boy, bats. He SWINGS and the
ball arcs high into the air and comes down--

ANGLE OUTFIELD - DAY

-- in Godwin's glove. Wearing his BASEBALL CAP BACKWARDS, he lobs the ball
to the shortstop.

EXT. PUBLIC SWIMMING POOL, DALLAS - DAY

Boys swim and engage in horseplay. Godwin swims laps.

Breathing hard, he pulls himself out of the deep end.

A SHAPELY WOMAN in a swimsuit passes. Godwin CHECKS HER OUT.

EXT. RIVERBANK NEAR DALLAS - DAY

Several BOYS fish with bamboo poles.

Nearby is Godwin, in sunglasses and a Colt .45 baseball cap, reading a COMIC. Hidden inside it is a paperback novel.

A boy jumps up and pulls off his shirt.

                    BOY
          Last one in's a shit-eating Yankee!

Godwin drops his comic, revealing "Seven Days In May." He pulls off his shirt and joins the dash into the water.

EXT. DALLAS TRINITY RIVER PARK - DAY

A crude TREE HOUSE is barely visible amid the foliage of a huge tree. JOEY carries a PAPER BAG as he climbs a rickety ladder to the tree house.

INT. TREE HOUSE - DAY

Several boys, including Godwin, sprawl on burlap sacks, looking at PLAYBOY MAGAZINES, passing a cigarette around. Joey reaches into the bag and pulls out TWO BOTTLES of LONE STAR BEER. Godwin reaches for a bottle opener on a string.

EXT. MOVIE THEATER - DAY

The marquee announces "Day of the Triffids."

INT. MOVIE THEATER - DAY

As large broccoli-like plants devour a woman, the young audience shrieks in mock horror. Godwin glances around, checking out all suspicious adults.

EXT. LIBERTY HIGH ATHLETIC FIELD - DAY

Boys throw and kick footballs.

Watching through the fence, Godwin turns and walks away.

INT. GODWIN'S APARTMENT - NIGHT

Eating Chinese takeout, Godwin watches "The Fugitive" on TV.

The stack of books is HIGHER.

EXT. LIBERTY HIGH SCHOOL - DAY

THE LEAVES ON trees lining the street ARE BEGINNING TO TURN.

Godwin ambles along the sidewalk, lost in thought.

Suddenly a BIG HAIRY HAND claps his shoulder.

                    TRUANT OFFICER
          You!

Godwin turns to see a barrel-chested man in a cheap suit.

                    GODWIN
          Yeah?

                    TRUANT OFFICER
          Why ain't you in school today?

                    GODWIN
          I don't live around here. I go to Crockett High in
          Irving.

                    TRUANT OFFICER
          So why ain't you there now?

                    GODWIN
          My grandpa lives around here -- but he just
          died. My folks went over to the funeral home. I
          just kind of wanted to walk around so I'll
          remember where Gramps used to live.

                    TRUANT OFFICER PATTERSON
          Which funeral home?

Godwin shrugs.

> TRUANT OFFICER PATTERSON (CONT'D)
> Sorry about your grandpa, but I've got to take
> you in. We'll call Crockett and straighten this
> out.

Godwin shrugs.

INT. LIBERTY HIGH - DAY

The truant officer escorts Godwin down the hall as the BELL RINGS. The corridor is flooded with KIDS.

Joey passes, SMILING at Godwin.

> JOEY
> Hey, Bobby!

The truant officer TIGHTENS his grip on Godwin's arm.

> TRUANT OFFICER PATTERSON
> Crockett High, my fanny.

INT. MEN'S VICE PRINCIPAL'S OFFICE - DAY

Godwin sits on a bench as Patterson paces.

The door opens for WALTER GILLETTE, 40s, dark and lean.

> GILLETTE
> Thank you, Mr. Patterson. Why don't you wait
> outside for a moment.

The truant officer leaves.

> GILLETTE (CONT'D)
> I don't put up with trouble makers.

> GODWIN
> I walk down a public street minding my own
> business when Mr. Mighty Joe Young mistakes
> me for a banana. So who's making trouble?

                    GILLETTE
There's no Robert Godwin registered here at
Liberty. Crockett High School never heard of
him. Now, what's your real name?

                    GODWIN
Robert Godwin.

                    GILLETTE
Tell me your name and let me speak to your
parent or guardian, or you're going with Mr.
Patterson.

                    GODWIN
Going where?

                    GILLETTE
The Dallas Youth Academy.

                    GODWIN
Reform school?

                    GILLETTE
Jail. Now, what's it gonna be?

Reluctantly, Godwin opens his wallet to get a slip of paper.

                    GODWIN
Let me call my aunt.

Gillette picks up the phone.

                    GILLETTE
What's the number?

EXT. LIBERTY JUNIOR HIGH - DAY

Godwin follows Debbie out the door and they get in a PICKUP.

INT. DEBBIE'S PICKUP TRUCK - DAY

Debbie drives, periodically glancing curiously at Godwin.

                    DEBBIE
    Well?

                    GODWIN
          I didn't think you were coming.

                    DEBBIE
          I was out of the office when they called. Would
          you like to tell me what's going on? Where's your
          dad?

                    GODWIN
          He died, a long time ago.

                    DEBBIE
          So who's looking after you?

                    GODWIN
          It's kind of a long story.

                    DEBBIE
          I've got time.

                    GODWIN
          Aren't you hungry?

EXT. EL FENIX FAMOUS MEXICAN RESTAURANT - DAY

White plates, brown booths, antique light bulbs. Men with faded jeans, checked
shirts and cowboy hats chow down.

Debbie watches Godwin expertly roll a fajita, then gobble it. As he chews he
LOOKS around the room carefully.

                    DEBBIE
          You were dead right.

                    GODWIN
          (mouth full) You don't believe a word of it?

                    DEBBIE
          I could almost buy a trust fund and a wicked
          uncle, but not the judge. It doesn't explain why
          you're in Texas. You need to be in Ohio.

                    GODWIN
          I figured. But I wanted you to get that I could
          whip up a whopper that any smart adult could
          puncture with a couple of phone calls.

                    DEBBIE
          (confused) Why's that?

                    GODWIN
          That's what a bright kid would do. But the truth
          is so bizarre that no child could dream it up. I
          want you to see that I know the difference.

Debbie sits back, arms folded.

                    DEBBIE
          This better be good. I had to take the whole day
          off from work.

                    GODWIN
          I'm a time traveler from the 21st century. I
          came back to stop the Kennedy assassination.

Debbie LAUGHS UPROARIOUSLY. Heads SWIVEL to watch her.

                    DEBBIE
          Lordy! And those 21st Century folks, the best
          they could do was send a skinny teenager!

                    GODWIN
          Absurd, isn't it?
          (BEAT)
          First of all, I wasn't sent. I came of my own
          volition. Second: I was born in 1950. When I left
          the 21st Century, I was 63 years old.
          (BEAT)
          When I arrived here last June, I was 13. Again.
          It was a big surprise. I was so frightened that I
          very nearly turned around and went back to my
          own time.

Debbie STARES, disbelieving but hooked.

                    DEBBIE
          Why didn't you?

                    GODWIN
          On one level, because I happened to arrive on
          the day that Kennedy's "Ich Bin Ein Berliner"
          speech was broadcast, and I saw again how
          much the man inspires ordinary Americans. But
          on another level --

I've been thinking about this for months -- it
might be because...

                    DEBBIE
Because?

                    GODWIN
Because I spent a lifetime in academia, playing it
safe. Avoiding risk. And...

                    DEBBIE
... you felt it was time to start taking a few
chances?

Godwin nods, THINKING.

                    GODWIN
Now, ask yourself -- is this a story that a
juvenile could come up with? Even a prodigy?

                    DEBBIE
You must have read it somewhere. Or maybe
you really believe that you're a 63-year-old man
in a little boy's body. In that case, you need a
head doctor.

                    GODWIN
You a baseball fan, Debbie?

                    DEBBIE
I don't much follow it.

                    GODWIN
In about two weeks the Dodgers play the
Yankees in the World Series.

                    DEBBIE
And *you* know who's gonna win.

                    GODWIN
The Dodgers sweep. Koufax pitches the first and
last games and is series MVP.

                    DEBBIE
I'll write that down and we'll see.

GODWIN

Debbie. Unless I can stop him, a man named Lee
Harvey Oswald will kill President Kennedy at
noon on November 22. Will you help me?

DEBBIE

Bobby, I really do like you. But I think you need
to see that head doctor.

GODWIN

If he's any good he'll conclude that I'm psychotic
and delusional. He'll lock me up and force me to
take powerful psychotropic drugs until I admit
that I'm sick.

DEBBIE

Is that what happened, Bobby? They put you in
a mental hospital?

GODWIN

No! Look, I didn't expect you to believe me. It's
much too fantastic. Frankly, I sometimes
wonder if I'm not asleep back in 2013, dreaming
all this.
(BEAT)
But thanks for helping me with the school. I'm
still learning to think like a kid again.

DEBBIE

What happened to your parents?

GODWIN

They died when I was five.

DEBBIE

How can you be so smart when you don't even
go to school?

GODWIN

You haven't been listening. I spent my
adolescence in a county orphanage. I graduated
high school at 17, then joined the Air Force. I
got out in 1971 and went to college on the GI
Bill. I'm a tenured professor at CalTech.

                    DEBBIE
          A professor! I suppose you have a PhD or
          something?

                    GODWIN
          One in history and another in electrical
          engineering.
          (SILLY GRIN)
          My friends say I'm a pair o' docs.

                    DEBBIE
          (GROANS at pun) Suppose I believe you. Why
          tell all this to *me*?

                    GODWIN
          Because now I know that I can't do this alone. I
          have to trust *somebody*, and you're the only
          adult that I can trust. Maybe.

Godwin LOOKS around the room.

                    DEBBIE
          Why do you keep looking around?

                    GODWIN
          The FBI, I think, is after me. I sent some letters
          warning about Oswald, but instead of looking
          for him, they're after me.

                    DEBBIE
          Bobby, I'm just a secretary. But my Uncle Ed is a
          real smart man, and he knows a lot of
          important people in Dallas. Maybe he could
          help?

Godwin nods appreciatively, then gets up.

                    GODWIN
          Good! We'll set up a meeting.
          (BEAT)
          Could you order me some flan while I use the
          mens room?

Debbie signals for a waiter as Godwin hurries off.

INT. EL FENIX, OUTSIDE MENS ROOM - DAY

Debbie waits.

The door opens and a WAITER comes out.

> WAITER
> No one is in there, senorita.

Debbie pushes the door open and SEES that the window is OPEN.

EXT. DALLAS AQUARIUM - DAY

Godwin is on a phone in a booth near the entrance.

> GODWIN
> Debbie, it's me. Has your uncle left yet?
> (BEAT)
> Good. Instead of the Fair Grounds, tell him to
> meet me at the Aquarium in one hour.
> (BEAT)
> By the Manatees.
> (BEAT)
> I'm wearing a Colt. 45 ball cap, *backwards*. And
> a Yankee T-shirt.

INT. DALLAS AQUARIUM - DAY

Godwin stares at the huge, playful mammals as they dive and swim around a lighted tank.

Through the tank appears the DISTORTED SHAPE of a MAN in a STETSON. The man WAVES.

> UNCLE ED
> Bobby? Is that you?

> GODWIN
> Stay there. I'll come around.

Godwin rounds the tank to SEE a figure half-hidden in shadow. Only the crown of his hat and his boots are clearly visible.

Snakeskin boots. The vamp of each boot is emblazoned with a STRIKING RATTLER BARING ITS FANGS.

> UNCLE ED
> Ed Coulter.

                    GODWIN
Robert Godwin.

             UNCLE ED (COL. COULTER)
let's go someplace where we can talk.

                    GODWIN
I like it fine right here.

                  COL. COULTER
That was quite a tale you spun for my niece,
Professor. Now, what's this about someone
killing the President?

                    GODWIN
So much for small talk. I wrote the Dallas police,
the FBI, the Secret Service and the Governor.

Nobody seems to care. Instead, they're coming
after *me*.

                  COL. COULTER
Put yourself in their shoes. They get a letter
from someone who knows more about the
President's plans than they do, they have to ask
themselves how that could be?
(BEAT)
Where's a fellow get information like that? What
kind of scheme is he trying to hatch?

                    GODWIN
Any schoolboy in 2013 knows every fact in
those letters.

                  COL. COULTER
But you've got to admit, most folks never meet
anyone from the 21st century. And if they did,
they wouldn't be talking about it.

                    GODWIN
So you think I'm a mental case.

                  COL. COULTER
My niece told me about your World Series
prediction.

I checked with some friends in Las Vegas and
they tell me about 600 people have already bet
on a Dodger sweep.

Did they *all* ride in with you from the 21st
century?

> GODWIN
>
> On November 1, President Diem of South
> Vietnam will be ousted in a coup d'état. Then
> murdered.

> COL. COULTER
>
> The president of *what?*

> GODWIN
>
> South Vietnam. It's near Thailand.

> COL. COULTER
>
> (Underwhelmed) Right.

> GODWIN
>
> And on November 6, a boy named Michael
> Douglas will be killed in a traffic collision. In
> Midland.

> COL. COULTER
>
> Why does anybody in 2013 care about some oil-
> patch traffic accident?

> GODWIN
>
> Because the driver of the other car, Laura
> Welch, will marry George Bush, who will become
> President of the United States.
>
> Unless you help me stop Kennedy's
> assassination.

> COL. COULTER
>
> Huh. Well, I'll look into it.

> GODWIN
>
> I'll be in touch.

Before Coulter can snatch him, Godwin vanishes into the shadows.

EXT. DALLAS AQUARIUM - DAY

Wearing a straw hat and a Six Flags T-shirt, Godwin tags along with a bunch of school kids walking to a SCHOOL BUS.

Dressed in casual clothes, Lundgren and Ficke sit in a white Volkswagen. They WATCH Godwin come around the school bus and amble toward a rack of bicycles.

He TAKES one and RIDES off. They don't react.

INT. COL. COULTER'S OFFICE - DAY

Coulter confronts his two musketeers.

                    COL COULTER
          You had to see it to believe it, boys. Kid four feet
          tall spouting Texas gushers o' five dollar words!
          Bucked him up when I called him professor!

                    LUNDGREN
          Could he really be a time traveler?

Ficke laughs, SLAPPING his knee, then WINCES.

                    COL COULTER
          You gone soft in the head?

Lundgren looks SHEEPISH.

                    COL COULTER (CONT'D)
          He had me for a minute. Then he starts talking
          about George Bush becoming President.

Lundgren and Ficke look expectant.

                    COL COULTER (CONT'D)
          I made a few calls. This Bush fellah's an offshore
          wildcatter outta Midland.
          His outfit and the CIA are thicker than ticks on
          a hound dog's nuts. He's fixing to run for US
          Senator next year.

          I'm no professor from 2013, but I know that he's
          gonna lose.

                    FICKE
Why's that, Colonel?

                    COL. COULTER
'cause he's a Republican carpet-bagger, 'bout as
Texas as clam chowder. His daddy was a Wall
Street banker -- US Senator from Connecticut.
Anyway, he's already got a wife and a passel of
pups. (BEAT) I'll tell you what's going on here,
boys. And it ain't pretty.

Coulter opens a desk drawer and takes out a worn paperback. He holds up
"The Manchurian Candidate," by Richard Condon.

                    LUNDGREN
Wasn't that a movie?

                    COULTER
(nods) Last year. Y'all go see it?

          Both Rangers shake their heads.

                    COULTER (CONT'D)
Me neither. But last night I read the book. It's
about mind control.

                    FICKE
Brainwashing?

                    COULTER
Yup. Now somebody has taken a smart little
orphan boy and used drugs and psychological
conditioning to turn him into a zombie who
thinks he's a professor from the year 2013.
Sickening.

                    LUNDGREN
Who could do that? And why?

                    COULTER
Whoever's pulling the strings knows too much
about America to be foreign. My money's on the
CIA. As for the why, look at what he wants us to
do: Arrest an innocent man, change the
President's motorcade route -- that sort of thing.

                    LUNDGREN
          So they kill Kennedy and we're set up to take the
          fall?

                    COULTER
          Go to the head of the class, Willy.

INT. DALLAS MUNICIPAL BUS - DAY

SUPER: NOVEMBER 7th, 1963

The bus is crowded with morning commuters.

Godwin STANDS, grasping a pole as LEE HARVEY OSWALD, 24, short and
slender with thinning brown hair and haunted EYES, comes down the aisle
carrying a BROWN LUNCH BAG. He stops near Godwin and grabs an overhead
strap.

Godwin is RIVETED.

The bus lurches. Oswald SEES Godwin staring at him.

                    OSWALD
          You lost or something? Need help?

Godwin shakes his head and looks away.

EXT. DEALEY PLAZA - DAY

The bus stops near a GRASSY KNOLL and several people get out. One is
Oswald. He heads toward the Texas Book Depository.

INT. DALLAS MUNICIPAL BUS - DAY

Godwin's face is against a window as he WATCHES Oswald ENTER the building.
He LOOKS UP at the sixth floor CORNER WINDOW.

INT. COL. COULTER'S OFFICE - DAY

Coulter's desk is covered with newspapers opened to STORIES about the Saigon
coup and Diem's murder. The SPEAKER BOX BUZZES.

                    SECRETARY (O.S.)
          Colonel, I have Chief Runyan.

Coulter picks up the phone.

> COL. COULTER
> How's tricks in Midland, Chief? Still hotter than
> Hades?
>
> Yeah, yeah, that's what I heard. You been
> keeping the peace and all?
>
> (CHUCKLES) I reckon. Say, Chief, reason for the
> call is I understand there was a traffic fatality
> last night? Boy name of Michael Douglas?
>
> Well, you know how it is. I have a few friends
> here and there.
>
> You have somebody in custody?
>
> Huh. Oh, it's like that. Sure, I understand. Can't
> buck that.
>
> No, nothing like that. I thought it might be
> connected to a case we're working, but no.
>
> Good to talk to you, chief. Keep on keeping on.

Coulter hangs up and rests his chin on his knuckles.

> COL. COULTER (CONT'D)
> I'll be a cross-eyed cocksucker.

INT. CORRIDOR OUTSIDE GODWIN'S APARTMENT - NIGHT

Godwin kneels at his door and carefully wedges a tiny WOOD SHAVING
between door and jamb. He PULLS the door shut.

He walks down the corridor.

EXT. DORA'S DINER - NIGHT

A greasy spoon in a blue-collar neighborhood.

INT. DORA'S DINER - NIGHT

Godwin and Debbie eye each other across a booth.

                    GODWIN
          What does your Uncle Ed think about me now?
          What do *you* think?

                    DEBBIE
          Tell me what you need him to do.

                    GODWIN
          The police could put an undercover officer into
          the Book Depository to watch Oswald.

          But really, there's no need for anyone to get
          hurt. No need to make orphans out of Oswald's
          kids.

          No need to make him a villain for the ages. All
          your uncle has to do is get someone to offer
          Oswald a good job a long way from Dallas.

          Keep him out of town until Kennedy's gone.

                    DEBBIE
          What if he doesn't want to leave?

                    GODWIN
          Make him an offer he can't refuse.

                    DEBBIE
          (charmed) You do have a way with words,
          Bobby.

                    GODWIN
          Not me. Mario Puzo.

INT. CORRIDOR OUTSIDE GODWIN'S APARTMENT - NIGHT

Godwin kneels at his door. The shaving is where he left it.

He takes out his key and goes inside.

EXT. DALLAS BUS - DAY

SUPER: NOVEMBER 20, 1963

A bus idles at a bus stop. Godwin gets on.

INT. BUS - DAY

As the bus pulls out, Godwin sits next to a MAN with a newspaper. On PAGE ONE is a map of JFK's MOTORCADE ROUTE.

The bus slows and stops. Passengers get on and off. Down the aisle comes Oswald. Godwin pulls his CAP LOW over his eyes.

EXT. PARK, DALLAS - NOON

Debbie sits on a bench feeding pigeons as Godwin arrives.

She SMILES as he sits beside her. She's very glad to see him.

                    GODWIN
          Debbie, he's still here.

                    DEBBIE
          Who is?

                    GODWIN
          Oswald. I saw him on the bus this morning. He
          got off at the book depository, just like always.

                    DEBBIE
          Uncle Ed still has some questions for you.

                    GODWIN
          (exasperated) What now?

                    DEBBIE
          Bobby, they want to know how you got here. Did
          you come in a spaceship? A time machine?
          How?

                    GODWIN
          I'm not sure I can put it in terms that you and
          Ed could understand.

                    DEBBIE
          Uncle Ed's friends don't want trouble. They're
          businessmen.

They don't understand how a 13-year-old boy is
able to survive in a big city all by himself.

Where do you get money for food? For clothes?
For your apartment?

Who helps you?

> GODWIN
> (annoyed) Weren't you listening? I'm NOT a kid.
> I planned my trip.

I brought money. I took precautions.

But I didn't anticipate that I'd revert to my 1963
age.

Godwin gets up from the bench.

> GODWIN
> We're running out of time.

> DEBBIE
> Have you had lunch?

> GODWIN
> Yes -- wait. A minute ago you said, "apartment"?
> How do you know that I have an apartment?

> DEBBIE
> I just assumed. I mean, you don't really need a
> *house*.

> GODWIN
> Oh, sure. Bye, Debbie.

He turns and DISAPPEARS into a crowd of lunchtime park-goers.

INT. CORRIDOR OUTSIDE GODWIN'S APARTMENT - NIGHT

Godwin kneels at his door. The tiny shaving is ON the floor. He puts an ear to
the door and LISTENS intently

INT. GODWIN'S APARTMENT - DAY

Godwin looks around. Everything SEEMS normal. He walks to the LAMP and takes out the bulb. Nothing.

Something catches his eye. He PEERS at A SPOT on the wall. It's not quite the SAME SHADE. He touches it with a finger.

PAINT comes off on his hand.

He JAMS a SCREW DRIVER into the wet spot. PLASTER FLIES.

He reaches into the hole and brings out a MICROPHONE.

EXT. HUNTER APARTMENTS - DAY

Carrying an overnight bag and a shopping bag, Godwin hurries down the fire escape.

EXT. ALLEY BEHIND HUNTER APARTMENTS - DAY

Godwin cautiously peers around the corner and SEES two men in a parked white Volkswagen: Lundgren and Ficke.

He turns and heads the other way, then opens A WALKWAY GATE.

INT. COL. COULTER'S OFFICE - NIGHT

Furious, Coulter paces in front of the desk. He turns to confront Lundgren and Ficke as they enter.

> COL. COULTER
> Gone? Slipped away with TWO Texas Rangers
> watching his place?

Ficke starts to speak and Lundgren STEPS on his foot.

> COL. COULTER (CONT'D)
> What spooked him?

ANOTHER ANGLE ON OFFICE

Clad in a tailored blue suit, Debbie, rises from a chair. Her hair is pulled into a tight bun. On her purse strap: A San Antonio Police Department BADGE.

                    DEBBIE
He seemed a little nervous in the park. I might
have slipped -- I mentioned that he had an
apartment.

                    COL. COULTER
You damn fool!

Lundgren and Ficke relax, glad that it's *her* under the gun.

                    DEBBIE
I think we need to bring him in.

                    COL. COULTER
(mimics) We need to bring him in!

Get his picture to the Dallas department.
Wanted for questioning.

EXT. DALLAS TRINITY RIVER PARK - NIGHT

A thicket. High above is the TREE HOUSE. Joey gets off his bike carrying a
laundry bag. He stars up the ladder.

INT. TREE HOUSE - NIGHT

Newspapers taped across windows. A bed of burlap sacks. Godwin in a BLACK
SWEATSHIRT and a watch cap.

In the hissing light of a Coleman lantern, Joey pulls a paper sack out of the
laundry bag, followed by a water jug.

                    JOEY
Hope you like tuna.

Godwin opens the bag, unwraps a sandwich and starts to eat.

EXT. DALLAS TRINITY RIVER PARK - NIGHT

Godwin and Joey shake hands. Godwin climbs onto the bike.

                    JOEY
Why can't I come with you?

                    GODWIN
          It's a three-hour ride, one way.

                    JOEY
          I told you. We could take my Dad's car. He won't
          even miss it.

                    GODWIN
          What if he does? And reports it stolen? It's too
          chancy.

                    JOEY
          Yeah, I guess.

                    GODWIN
          Thanks for everything, Joey. And don't forget
          what I told you.

                    JOEY
          I wrote it down: Microsoft, and Apple.

Joey watches Godwin peddle away. Then he takes his baseball cap and turns it
around BACKWARDS.

EXT. PAINE RESIDENCE, IRVING, TEXAS - NIGHT

A tract house with detached garage. In the yard, a mature tree abuts the
garage.

WALKING the bike, Godwin stops and leans the bike against the tree. He walks
slowly around the garage.

He tries the side door. Locked.

He tries the pull-down garage door. Locked.

He walks behind the garage and sees a LOUVERED WINDOW at the apex of the
peaked roof.

He stands on the bicycle and climbs into the tree.

EXT. ROOF OF PAINE GARAGE - NIGHT

Hanging from a tree limb, Godwin LOWERS himself to the roof.

He hangs over the edge and sticks a skinny arm through the louvered window. He pops a SLAT and brings it up. Another.

INT. GARAGE - NIGHT

Godwin squeezes through the window and climbs down the exposed 2 x 4s of the frame. He takes out a tiny FLASHLIGHT and pans the space, revealing a dozen BIG cardboard BOXES.

A DOG barks nearby.

A BABY WAILS from inside the Paine house.

Godwin finds a BUNDLE wrapped with drapes behind a big box next to the water heater.

It's tied with heavy cord. He lays it on the floor and unties the cord revealing...

A RIFLE with a Mauser action.

Godwin tries to remove the bolt as the gun store salesman did, but the mount for the telescopic sight is in the way.

An ENGINE is heard. A CAR STOPS outside the garage.

A car door SLAMS.

FOOTSTEPS CRUNCH on GRAVEL.

SOMEONE TRIES the SIDE DOOR. LOCKED. The FOOTSTEPS RETREAT.

Godwin rolls the bundle up and stashes it behind the heater.

THE DOOR OPENS. The LIGHT comes on. GODWIN HIDES in a corner.

A YOUNG MAN ENTERS and LOOKS AROUND. He steps outside.

> MICHAEL (O.C.)
> Ruth, how the hell am I supposed to find
> anything in here?

> RUTH (O.C.)
> Shhh! You'll wake the baby! Come in and tell me
> what you're looking for.

Michael exits, leaving the light on and the door open.

Godwin climbs back up the wall and out through the window.

EXT. GARAGE ROOF - NIGHT

Godwin peeps down to see Michael rummaging through boxes, sorting papers, carrying items to the parked car.

It's plain that he'll be busy for hours.

Godwin climbs down the tree, wheels the bike into the alley and silently peddles away.

EXT. DEALEY PLAZA - DAY

Workers set up police BARRICADES along the motorcade route.

Early arrivals stake out their places behind the barricades.

A cute tween-age GIRL CHEWING bubble gum and carrying a shopping bag picks her way down the sidewalk. As she PASSES a COP she blows a bubble so huge it obscures her face.

A ROTUND, BOSOMY woman minding several children FROWNS.

> FROWNING WOMAN
> Young lady!

The girl TURNS. It's Godwin in a DRESS AND WIG.

> FROWNING WOMAN (CONT'D)
> Chewing gum is a filthy habit.

Godwin shrugs and turns away.

Amused, a flashily dressed young woman CRACKS her gum.

> GUM CHEWING WOMAN
> Beats chewing your cud, Elsie.

She elbows the man standing next to her.

SQUINTING after Godwin, the man pushes his hat back, revealing his face: Travis.

> TRAVIS
> Just mind your own business.

He WATCHES Godwin turn the corner.

EXT. TEXAS BOOK DEPOSITORY - DAY

Passing Ficke to enter the building, Godwin blows a bubble.

EXT. LOVE FIELD, OUTSIDE DALLAS - DAY

The PRESIDENTIAL MOTORCADE leaves the airport. KENNEDY rides in the back seat of an open-top limo, his WIFE beside him. In the front passenger seat are GOVERNOR and MRS. CONNALLY.

SECRET SERVICE OFFICERS ride running boards as the motorcade ZIPS along at 30 mph.

INT. TEXAS BOOK DEPOSITORY - DAY

Godwin SMILES at a uniformed security guard.

                    SECURITY GUARD
          Where are you going, Missy?

                    GODWIN
          My dad -- Mr. Jarman -- he said it would be
          okay if I watched the motorcade from the fifth
          floor?

The guard smiles and WAVES Godwin through.

INT. SIXTH FLOOR OF TEXAS BOOK DEPOSITORY - DAY

The wig and dress are gone. In a BAGGY SWEATSHIRT over jeans Godwin enters a large room stacked high with packing boxes.

Nobody is around.

Godwin looks around, spots the rifle, still wrapped. He unwraps it, pulls the bolt back, revealing a full magazine. He tilts the rifle down, exposing an empty chamber. He takes the BUBBLE GUM and with his fingers rolls it into a ball.

He starts to put the gum in the chamber.

A HAND grabs his shoulder.

                              OSWALD
               Careful, son. That's a real gun.

Godwin turns to FIND Oswald.

                         OSWALD (CONT'D)
               What are you doing here?

He TAKES the rifle from Godwin and CHAMBERS a round.

                              GODWIN
               What are *YOU* doing here? Why do you have a
               rifle, Mr. Oswald? Who are you going to shoot?
               The president?

                              OSWALD
               How do you know my name?

                              GODWIN
               Mr. Oswald, don't do this. Don't make Marina a
               widow.

               Don't damn your own children with the mark of
               Cain! I know what that's like -- please, walk
               away now.

                              OSWALD
               What are you talking about? I ain't gonna hurt
               nobody.

                              GODWIN
               Not even President Kennedy?

                              OSWALD
               (laughs) Oh, no. See, I used to be a Marine. And
               you know what they say—and it's true, there are
               no *ex*-marines.

               Anyway, I'm here to *protect* the president, is all.

                              GODWIN
               You're here to kill Kennedy. If you do, by
               Monday you'll be dead too.

                              OSWALD
               Why don't I buy you a coke and we'll talk about
               it?

Twisting Godwin's arm behind his back, Oswald steers him toward a steel door.

He opens the door, revealing a closet. He SHOVES Godwin inside.

EXT. MOTORCADE ROUTE IN SUBURB OUTSIDE DALLAS - DAY

The motorcade STOPS and Kennedy HOPS OUT to EMBRACE a NUN and shake hands with several uniformed CATHOLIC SCHOOL STUDENTS.

INT. BOOK DEPOSITORY, SIXTH FLOOR - DAY

Oswald shoves several boxes together near the open CORNER WINDOW to form a crude shooting stand.

INT. CLOSET - DAY

The room is dark except for a FAINT SHAFT of LIGHT near the ceiling.

Godwin hunts around and finds a light switch. The light reveals many BUNDLES of flattened corrugated BOXES.

Godwin POUNDS on the door.

                    GODWIN
          Let me out! Help! Help!

He pauses to listen and hears only thick spongy SILENCE.

Godwin looks UP TO SEE a GAP between ceiling and wall.

He looks around, measures a bundle's thickness with his hands, then eyes the wall, silently counting.

He begins DRAGGING bundles to line them up on the floor.

EXT. MOTORCADE ROUTE NEAR DOWNTOWN DALLAS - DAY

The motorcade SLOWS to thread through THRONGS of CHEERING PEOPLE spilling off the sidewalks into the STREET.

INT. CLOSET - DAY

Godwin has built a STEPPED RAMP of bundles.

PERSPIRING, he climbs to the top and pulls himself UP.

He DROPS a bundle to see how long it takes to hit the floor.

He shoves a bundle through the crack. Listens to compare how long it takes to hit the UNSEEN FLOOR outside.

INT. BOOK DEPOSITORY, FIRE STAIRWELL - DAY

Hanging by his fingertips, Godwin DROPS to the stairs, his landing cushioned by the bundle of corrugated boxes.

He tries the DOOR. Locked. He runs down a flight of stairs.

INT. BOOK DEPOSITORY, SIXTH FLOOR - DAY

Oswald looks through the window at flags fluttering from poles around Dealey Plaza.

Fingers at arm's length, he gauges the wind speed, then adjusts the rifle's telescopic sight.

INT. BOOK DEPOSITORY, FIRE STAIRWELL - DAY

Godwin finds the fifth floor door LOCKED.

EXT. REAR OF BOOK DEPOSITORY BUILDING - DAY

A steel door opens and Godwin appears. He sprints off.

EXT. STREET NEXT TO TEXAS BOOK DEPOSITORY - DAY

As people lining the street CRANE THEIR NECKS, Godwin runs out of the alley. He COLLIDES with Travis.

                    TRAVIS
            Going somewhere, Bobby?

He PUNCHES Godwin, bloodying his LIP. Travis then GAGS him with a SCARF and, looking around, DRAGS him toward the alley.

EXT. MAIN STREET, DALLAS - DAY

Led by motorcycle police, the motorcade turns into Houston Street to CHEERS and THUNDEROUS APPLAUSE.

Secret Service agents EYE rooftops and SCAN the crowd.

In the Presidential limo's front passenger seat, an ELATED Mrs. Connally swivels to face Kennedy.

> MRS. CONNALLY
> Mr. President, you can't say Dallas doesn't love
> you!

INT. BOOK DEPOSITORY, SIXTH FLOOR - DAY

Oswald SQUINTS through the telescopic sight.

ANGLE MOTORCADE, OSWALD'S P.O.V. THROUGH SCOPE - CONTINUOUS

Following the cycles and a closed COMMAND CAR, JFK's open-topped limo swims into FOCUS.

The CROSS-HAIRS move until they rest on Kennedy's head. The car comes CLOSER and CLOSER.

EXT. ALLEY BEHIND BOOK DEPOSITORY - DAY

Travis throws Godwin to the pavement. He takes out a KNIFE.

> TRAVIS
> Tell me where Lucy went or I'll cut your little
> nuts off.

Godwin reaches under his sweatshirt and pulls out a .45 AUTOMATIC. POINTING it with two hands, he slowly gets up. Then spits out the scarf.

> GODWIN
> I don't have time for this. Get out of my way or
> I'll kill you.

QUICK AS A COBRA, Travis LUNGES at GODWIN and GRABS the GUN.

It BREAKS in two, revealing a painted balsa wood FAKE.

> TRAVIS
> (laughs) Man! Thought it was real.

Godwin dodges past Travis, who grabs his sweatshirt and jerks him off his feet.

From the street comes APPLAUSE and CHEERS, rising to a DEAFENING CRESCENDO.

> TRAVIS (CONT'D)
> Screw Lucy!

He LUNGES with the knife. Godwin rolls away, tripping Travis. Travis FALLS but as Godwin gets up, Travis grabs him again. He gets to his feet LIFTING him by the neck to eye level.

> TRAVIS (CONT'D)
> Now I gut you like the little piggie that you are.

As he COCKS his arm, a SHOT rings out. Then ANOTHER.

A THIRD SHOT, much CLOSER.

Travis drops Godwin, falling to his knees, blood oozing from the WOUND in his BICEPS. He WRITHES in pain. His hat and a cheap TOUPEE have fallen, revealing a burn-scarred head.

From the street nearby comes the sound of SIRENS, a COMMOTION, people SCREAMING and RUNNING past the alley.

Godwin gets up to see FICKE, still in a SHOOTING STANCE.

Ficke holsters his pistol and walks over to Travis.

> TRAVIS (CONT'D)
> I'm bleeding! Get me a doctor, man!

> FICKE
> You'll live. Not so sure about your hair,
> though...

He CUFFS Travis to a STANDPIPE, then takes out a BUSINESS CARD and STUFFS it in the pimp's shirt pocket.

> GODWIN
> Texas Rangers!?

Ficke nods, PROUD.

                    GODWIN (CONT'D)
Listen carefully! In two minutes Oswald leaves
the building. Take him now and he won't kill
Officer Tippit.

EXT. TEXAS BOOK DEPOSITORY - DAY

Oswald leaves by the front door. He's not in a hurry.

                    FICKE (V.O.)
My orders were to find *you*. If Oswald fired
those shots, Dallas PD will handle it.

Oswald boards a bus and it pulls away.

EXT. ALLEY BEHIND BOOK DEPOSITORY - DAY

Godwin tries to RUN but Ficke SHOVES him against a wall. Godwin BREAKS
DOWN, anger and frustration bubbling over.

                    FICKE
That's right, cry. Get it out. You'll feel better.

                    GODWIN
(nearly incoherent)
Sonsabitches! Call yourself police! ...
Unbelievable! Stupid bozos!

I gave you *everything* -- when, where, who -- I
even told you how to neutralize -- What the hell
is the matter with you people?

                    TRAVIS
(to Ficke) That was my boy, I'd have to slap him
upside the head and teach him some manners.

Ficke is AMUSED. Godwin turns a COLD GAZE on Travis.

                    GODWIN
President Kennedy's dead, and you, who learned
your manners — where, pimp school? — want
to discuss the social graces?

                    TRAVIS
(STRICKEN) The President's dead?

                              FICKE
                    Let's go, Professor.

INT. INTERROGATION ROOM - DAY

A starkly illuminated room with a table, two chairs. A wall clock that reads
1:00. On one wall is a large ONE-way MIRROR.

Ficke ENTERS, TRIUMPHANT, pushing Godwin in front of him.

He shoves Godwin in a chair, CUFFS him to the table, leaves.

Godwin PULLS his slender wrist free of the manacle and approaches the
mirror.

                              GODWIN
                    Listen carefully -- there's no time to waste!
                    President Kennedy is dead. But in about 15
                    minutes--

INT. OBSERVATION ROOM - CONTINUOUS

Ficke joins Coulter, Lundgren and Debbie OBSERVING Godwin talking to the
window.

                    GODWIN (CONTINUED)
                    -- a Dallas police officer named J.D. Tippet will
                    get out of a radio car near 10th and Patton.

                    Oswald will kill him. For the love of God, don't
                    let it happen!

                         COL. COULTER
                    Nice job with the handcuffs, Ficke.
                         (BEAT)
                    Look at him. Not a sign of emotion. Like a robot.
                    Probably drugs. Maybe sleep deprivation.

Ficke LOOKS like he WANTS to speak, but changes his mind.

INT. INTERROGATION ROOM - DAY

Coulter enters to put a Coke and a burger on the table.

                    COL. COULTER
          Figured you might be hungry.

                    GODWIN
          So it's your turn to play good cop. "Uncle Ed."

                    COL. COULTER
          It's *Colonel* Ed Coulter. And if I had my druthers
          I'd as soon shove my boot right up your ass
          right now.

                    GODWIN
          Your good-cop routine's a little rusty, isn't it?

Coulter SLAMS his FIST on the table.

                    COL. COULTER
          You're in a shitload of trouble, boy.

                    GODWIN
          (LAUGHS) You going to sit there and blow
          smoke at me, or are you going do your job and
          save Officer Tippit?

Coulter BACKHANDS Godwin, bloodying his nose.

                    COL. COULTER
          Don't *you* tell me what my job is!

                    GODWIN
          You must be proud of yourself -- a grown man
          beating up on a kid.

Abashed, Coulter hands Godwin a handkerchief and leaves.

INT. TEXAS RANGERS OFFICES, COURTHOUSE - DAY

Pulling himself together, Coulter walks down the corridor and stops outside an
office.

He looks around and SEES secretaries WEEPING, Lundgren and Ficke
CONSOLING each other. Ficke PUNCHES a WALL.

Coulter sticks his head into an office.

                    COL. COULTER
          I'll take that file, Emily.

ASHEN-FACED, EMILY hands him a manila folder.

> EMILY
> I just can't believe he's dead.

INT. INTERROGATION ROOM - DAY

Coulter enters carrying the file to find Godwin pacing.

The food and drink are untouched. The clocks says 1:20.

> COL. COULTER
> We'll start over.

> GODWIN
> So I may assume that you did nothing to save
> Officer Tippit?

> COL. COULTER
> *I* ask the questions here.

Godwin purses his lips, shaking his head in frustration.

> GODWIN
> I assert my rights under the Constitution. I
> want an attorney present while I'm questioned.

Off a LOOK by COULTER.

> GODWIN (CONT'D)
> The law says you *must* provide me with an
> attorney.

> COL. COULTER
> Damn it boy, you're in Texas. Far as you're
> concerned, I *am* the law.

> GODWIN
> As a minor, you have no legal basis to question
> me without a parent or guardian present.

With a SNEER, Coulter takes a SHEET of PAPER from the file.

> COL. COULTER
> Well, then, why don't I just call your parents?

                    GODWIN
My parents are dead.

                    COL. COULTER
That's right. Got it all here. In 1955 your daddy,
Gustaf Gottwin, a physicist, was questioned
about contacts with a suspected Russian agent.

Abandoned his family and went home to Prague.
Then your poor mom, Lena, killed herself.

Huh. Seems like bullshit never falls too far from
the bull.

Godwin looks STRICKEN.

                    GODWIN
I was five years old!

In 1955, that accusation alone was enough to
ruin your life. Dad was trying to spare us an
ordeal... He died two years later.

                    COL. COULTER
According to Penbrook Orphanage, when you
ran away last June, you were a ward of the state
of Ohio.

I don't imagine anybody will put up a stink
about me questioning a runaway suspected of
conspiracy.

                    GODWIN
Conspiracy?

                    COL. COULTER
Conspiracy to commit murder.

                    GODWIN
A conspiracy requires more than one. With
whom did I conspire?

                    COL. COULTER
That's what you're gonna tell me.

Godwin ROLLS his eyes.

                    GODWIN
          I thought you were smarter than this.

Coulter opens the file and takes out photos of Godwin's apartment with the
wall charts.

                    COL. COULTER
          Exhibit A -- details of the planned murders.
          Times, dates, locations.

                    GODWIN
          Exactly what I sent to warn the FBI and the
          Governor's office.

Coulter holds up the plastic-wrapped letters.

                    COL. COULTER
          You didn't write these.

                    GODWIN
          Who says?

                    COL. COULTER
          Crime lab says the paper's not available in the
          USA. Nor the ink.

                    GODWIN
          It will be. In 2013. In fact, they've probably got
          some prototypes now. Call Xerox in California.

                    COL. COULTER
          Boy, that time-traveler dog just ain't gonna
          hunt.

          Last chance to do yourself some good. Who's
          behind this? The KGB? FBI? CIA? Did they drug
          you?

INT. OBSERVATION ROOM - CONTINUOUS

Ficke, Lundgren and Debbie watch the interrogation.

                    LUNDGREN
          Sure doesn't talk like a kid.

                    FICKE
Smarter than any kid I ever met.

                    DEBBIE
Maybe he's telling the truth. Maybe he's really a
professor from the 21st century.

                    FICKE
Don't ever let the colonel hear you say that.

INT. INTERROGATION ROOM - DAY

Godwin looks THOUGHTFUL.

                    GODWIN
Okay, you win. The man you want is Jack Ruby.

                    COL. COULTER
You're telling me that little Jew bastard from
the Carousel Club is involved in this?

                    GODWIN
Pick him up. Sweat him a few days.

                    COL. COULTER
You got to do a lot better than a punk like Jack
Ruby.

                    GODWIN
(furious) I gave you everything you needed to
stop an assassination and you did nothing!

There's going to be a holy stink of an inquiry --
the biggest investigation in this country since
John Wilkes Booth shot Abraham Lincoln.

And when the facts are known, you and the
Texas Rangers will be the laughing stocks of law
enforcement, the poster boys of official
incompetence.

                    COL. COULTER
We're done here. For now.

INT. OBSERVATION ROOM - CONTINUOUS

Ficke, Lundgren and Debbie watch Coulter exit the room.

After a beat, he joins them and drops the file on a table.

> COL. COULTER
> I thought you were on your way back to San
> Antone.

> DEBBIE
> I was thinking he might talk to me.

> COL. COULTER
> We got it under control.
> (BEAT)
> Couple of nights downstairs alone and he'll be
> whistlin' Dixie.

> DEBBIE
> He's just a child, Colonel.

> COL. COULTER
> Officer Horton, I've been thinking.
> You'd make one fine Texas Ranger.

> DEBBIE
> (off guard) Uh, I didn't know women could
> apply?

> COL. COULTER
> Only because the right one hadn't come along
> yet. ¿Comprende?

Coulter extends his hand, a courtly gesture. She shakes it.

Nodding to Ficke and Lundgren, she leaves the room.

Coulter GLARES through the one-way glass at Godwin.

> LUNDGREN
> Give us an hour with him, Colonel.

> COL. COULTER
> Too late for that. *One* thing that little
> peckerhead said that rang true -- it gets out that
> we had all this and sat on it...

Ficke and Lundgren exchange glances.

EXT. CORRIDOR OUTSIDE OBSERVATION ROOM - DAY

Debbie waits for the elevator.

Suddenly she REALIZES that she doesn't have her purse. She turns and starts back. She pauses at the door, LISTENING.

> LUNDGREN (O.C.)
> What are we going to do?

> COL. COULTER (O.C.)
> I think we're gonna get lucky.
> (BEAT)
> He'll run off again tonight.
> (BEAT)
> Someplace nobody'll ever find him.

Debbie KNOCKS on the door, then enters.

INT. OBSERVATION ROOM - CONTINUOUS

Off a tense LOOK from Coulter.

> DEBBIE
> Forgot my purse, Colonel.

> COL. COULTER
> And I thought that was Ficke's!

Lundgren laughs. After a beat, Ficke joins in.

The PHONE RINGS. OFF a LOOK from Coulter, Lundgren answers.

> LUNDGREN
> Lundgren.
> (BEAT)
> Yeah, he's right here.
> (BEAT)
> Uh huh... Uh huh... Um, what was that name?

Ashen, he hangs up.

> COL. COULTER
> Well?

> LUNDGREN
> Governor Connally is gonna be okay.

Oswald is in custody, but not 'till he'd shot a
guy from Dallas PD.

                    COL. COULTER
And?

                    LUNDGREN
And an Officer Tippit, Dallas PD, was D.O.A. at
Methodist Hospital.

All four turn and STARE at Godwin through the glass.

                    COL. COULTER
Take him downstairs, boys.

I'll be on the lookout for your application,
Officer Horton.

He HANDS Debbie the FILE

                    COL. COULTER (CON'T)
Would you mind giving this to Emily on your
way out?

Debbie takes the file and leaves.

INT. COURTHOUSE BASEMENT - DAY

An old-fashioned dungeon three stories below street level.

High stone ceilings, steel doors, echoing cobblestone floors, row upon row of
dusty, empty cells. Rats scamper around.

In one cell Godwin lies on a bunk, shivering on bare bed springs. He HEARS
the faint sound of a door clanging shut.

After a beat, another door, closer. Then a third door, much closer. Hearing
footsteps, Godwin sits up.

Debbie appears on the other side of the bars. She hands him a sandwich and a
carton of milk.

                    DEBBIE
Not even a blanket?

                    GODWIN
          They're trying to soften me up for the next
          round of questioning.

                    DEBBIE
          Bobby, they're done asking questions.

She lets this sink in.

                    GODWIN
          So now I'm an embarrassment?

                    DEBBIE
          A liability. You know too much. They're afraid
          you could send them all to jail.

                    GODWIN
          So it's your turn to play good cop again.

                    DEBBIE
          Bobby, listen to me. I'm a San Antonio police
          officer. A rookie. I was a decoy, working a White
          Slavery case at the bus station.

          My sergeant told me to get on the bus and make
          friends with you.

                    GODWIN
          That's why they took the Mexican man off the
          bus?

                    DEBBIE
          That Mexican was Sgt. Jimenez, my boss.

          Anyway, when you called my number, they flew
          me up to Dallas to work your case.

                    GODWIN
          That's why it took you so long to pick me up at
          that school!

                    DEBBIE
          (takes his file out of her purse) I want to help
          you. Is there anything you can think of that
          would give Coulter a reason to let you live?

                    GODWIN
Does that mean you believe me?

                    DEBBIE
I just don't want them to kill you.

                    GODWIN
Can I see my file?

She passes the file through the bars. He reads at an incredible clip, flipping a page every few seconds. She watches, open-mouthed as he breezes through the file. Then he goes back and hands two sheets to Debbie.

                    DEBBIE
This is the incident report at the Alamo. And this is a Dayton PD blotter entry when Penbrook reported you missing from class.

                    GODWIN
Are the dates and times accurate?

                    DEBBIE
No reason to suppose they're not.

                    GODWIN
Would you swear under oath that those are official records that state the date and time accurately?

                    DEBBIE
Yes, of course.

                    GODWIN
Very well. What does it say about the day I went missing?

                    DEBBIE
(reads) On June 24, 1963, you answered third period roll at 10:00 am but missed fourth period at 11:00.

                    GODWIN
So I disappeared sometime between ten and eleven. When was I taken into custody at the Alamo?

                    DEBBIE
          (reads other paper) At 10:12 am.

Debbie looks up, confused.

                    DEBBIE (CONT'D)
          On June 24! That *can't* be right.

                    GODWIN
          A minute ago you were ready to swear under
          oath that it was.

                    DEBBIE
          I don't understand.

                    GODWIN
          You said that you believe that 12 minutes after I
          was seen in Dayton, I turned up in San Antonio.

          Then why you can't believe that I traveled back
          in time from 2013?

WIDE EYED, Debbie moves her mouth but no sound comes out.

                    GODWIN (CONT'D)
          I came to 1963 to try to change the world. Now
          all that I can do is try to save myself. Will you
          help me?

EXT. TIMBER GLENN BRANCH, DALLAS PUBLIC LIBRARY - NIGHT

The back door is open a crack. Inside the darkened building a   beam of light
dances inside a first-floor window.

INT. TIMBER GLENN BRANCH, DALLAS PUBLIC LIBRARY - NIGHT

A dark figure prowls the cavernous room, occasionally using a FLASHLIGHT.
Abruptly the flashlight goes one way and the figure tumbles to the floor,
scattering BOOKS.

                    DEBBIE
          Ow!

Debbie gets up, finds the flashlight and sees that she tripped over a stack of
books. She plays the light over the wall until she finds a door marked "LOST
AND FOUND."

INT. LOST AND FOUND - NIGHT

A windowless room. The flashlight moves over shelves with umbrellas, backpacks, briefcases, hats, eyeglasses, galoshes, books, canes, a wooden leg and bags of every description.

Debbie flips a light switch. A flash. The bulb's burned out. Using the flashlight, she begins to hunt through the bags.

INT. UNCLE RED'S FRIED CHICKEN - NIGHT

Dark and smoky. Ficke and Lundgren are the only white folks. Their table is covered by a sea of chicken bones and plates.

Lundgren LOOKS at a wall clock: 12:40.

>   FICKE
> I'm thinking we take the 660 out past Ferris. Lot
> of side roads...

Sure wish it hadn't come to this.

>   LUNDGREN
> Him or us. Come to a pissing contest with the
> Colonel, who do you think they're gonna
> believe?

>   FICKE
> Yeah. Yeah. I guess...

>   LUNDGREN
> Courthouse'll be nice and quiet.

They get up and Lundgren puts money on the table.

>   FICKE
> I've got a belly ache.

>   LUNDGREN
> Feels something like a flock of chickens?

INT. LIBRARY LOST AND FOUND - NIGHT

Debbie stands on a box and on tiptoe pulls a bag down from the top shelf. It's HEAVIER than she thought and she DROPS it and the flashlight, which goes out.

Outside the room something GOES THUD. She goes to the door and opens it a crack. A gaunt CAT rubs against her leg.

                    DEBBIE
          (whispers) I bet you're hungry.

Debbie turns around.

She SEES a FAINT, GHOSTLY BLUE GLOW emanating from the bag that she dropped.

EXT. OLD RED COURTHOUSE, DALLAS - NIGHT

Ficke and Lundgren get out of a car parked near a side entrance. Ficke carries a BIG POTATO SACK.

INT. OLD RED COURTHOUSE, DALLAS - NIGHT

The corridors are silent and lit only by fire lights as Lundgren and Ficke enter a big, high-ceilinged room at the center of a half-dozen corridors and stairwells.

Lundgren opens a door under a stairwell.

                    FICKE
          Hold on.

Off a LOOK by LUNDGREN.

                    FICKE (CONT'D)
          Got a little business to take care of. Down the
          hall.

                    LUNDGREN
          Now?

                    FICKE
          Ever have to use the crapper in a colored joint?

Lundgren shakes his head and they move off down the hall, turning a corner and out of sight.

After a BEAT Debbie enters, carrying Godwin's bag. Quietly, she opens the door under the stairwell.

INT. COURTHOUSE BASEMENT - NIGHT

A naked bulb hanging from the ceiling of Godwin's cell is the only light.

Somewhere nearby, a door SLAMS.

Debbie hurries across echoing cobblestones to Godwin.

> DEBBIE
> Ficke and Lundgren are upstairs!

> GODWIN
> The clothes!

Godwin strips, then struggles into adult-sized clothing.

> GODWIN (CONT'D)
> Now, the Device.

As the distant SOUND of a door SLAM echoes, Debbie takes the device out and TRIES to pass it through the bars. It's a bit too WIDE. Debbie turns it sideways. No dice.

Another door SLAMS. FOOTSTEPS ARE heard. Debbie TREMBLES.

> DEBBIE
> If they find me down here--

> GODWIN
> Open the door of the Device and hold the front
> against the bars.

Debbie presses the GEARED face against the steel.

A THIRD DOOR SLAMS, much closer.

> DEBBIE
> (softly) Sweet Jesus, save us!

Godwin checks the battery, then turns the FIRST gear. FOOTSTEPS ECHO in the darkness.

> FICKE (O.C.)
> Hey, professor! Bet you're hungry!

Godwin pushes the lever, once.

                    GODWIN
          (whispers) Hold it tight!

As the footsteps get LOUDER, Debbie HOLDS the wooden case.

GRIPPING the case, Godwin PRESSES the lever a second time.

A LONG BEAT

Ficke and Lundgren appear, a strip of toilet paper trailing from Ficke's
trousers.

Lundgren raises a ring of KEYS.

                    LUNDGREN
          We came to take you out to--

ANGLE FICKE AND LUNDGREN'S P.O.V. - CONTINUOUS

**The air SHIMMERS. A stocking FLOATS to the floor inside the cell. The
cell is EMPTY but for boy's clothing.**

                    LUNDGREN
          Is that frost?

Lundgren touches a steel bar, then JERKS his hand away.

                    LUNDGREN (CONT'D)
          I don't fucking believe this.

                    FICKE
          What now?

                    LUNDGREN
          I guess we get rid of his clothes.

                    FICKE
          What do we tell the Colonel?

                    LUNDGREN
          We tell anyone about this, ever, they lock us
          both in the loony bin.

INT. COURTHOUSE BASEMENT, GODWIN'S CELL - DAY

The light is OUT. Only a faint glow from a window high on the wall illuminates Godwin, still a boy, as he climbs to his feet. Groggy, he peers through the bars but SEES no one.

                    GODWIN
          Debbie? Officer Horton?

Silence.

                    GODWIN (CONT'D)
          (LOUDER) Debbie! Debbie!

A GROAN is heard in the gloom. Disheveled and dusty but still clutching the Device, Debbie comes up on WOBBLY legs.

                    GODWIN (CONT'D)
          You okay?

                    DEBBIE
          I'll do. What just happened?

                    GODWIN
          We couldn't move through space, so I moved us
          through time. It should be sometime Sunday
          morning.

                    DEBBIE
          You're scaring me.

                    GODWIN
          You've only lost one day out of your life. Now, I
          need to get out of this cell.

                    DEBBIE
          There must be a set of keys somewhere in the
          building.

                    GODWIN
          Forget that. Where's your car?

EXT. OLD RED COURTHOUSE - DAY

Debbie arrives at her car to find a PARKING TICKET on the windshield. She SEES a sign: "No Parking Sunday."

She ignores the ticket and opens the trunk.

INT. COURTHOUSE BASEMENT, GODWIN'S CELL - DAY

A JACK is wedged between bars. With EFFORT, Godwin turns the crank. As
the jack expands, the bars slowly BEND OUTWARD.

                    GODWIN
          In about two hours, Jack Ruby will shoot
          Oswald in the parking garage under Dallas
          police headquarters.

                    DEBBIE
          The guy you told Coulter to arrest?

Godwin pauses to WIPE sweat from his face, then continues to turn the crank.
The space between the bars SLOWLY WIDENS.

                    GODWIN
          Ruby has cancer.

          In four years, he'll die. In jail.

                    DEBBIE
          You were trying to save Oswald?

                    GODWIN
          To learn WHY he shot Kennedy.

                    DEBBIE
          Bobby, if this is a time machine, why come back
          here? What's so significant about Kennedy?

                    GODWIN
          Next week at Kennedy's funeral, leaders from all
          over the world will come to pay their respects.

          That's because after we Americans won World
          War II, we rebuilt Japan and Germany -- our
          former enemies!

          We're admired everywhere -- America is a beacon
          of hope to oppressed people around the world.

                    DEBBIE
          You sound like a history professor.

GODWIN

Thanks. Unfortunately, all that's about to change.

The new President, Johnson, will want to be reelected next year.

He won't want to look soft on Communism, so he'll plunge us into a senseless war.

Over a million Vietnamese civilians will be killed.

Our Army will be demoralized and our country will be divided. Over the next ten years, all the good will we earned after World War II will be squandered.

By 2003, we'll be involved in still another unjust war, and America will be reviled, not admired.

If you could see America 50 years from now, you wouldn't know it.

DEBBIE

Things would be that much different if Kennedy hadn't been killed?

Godwin takes the jack out from the bars, removes his jacket, and squeezes out of the cell. He mops his face on his sleeve.

GODWIN

From the perspective of 2013, you can draw direct parallels between Johnson's trumped-up rationale for going to war in Vietnam and the deceptions used to justify our invasion of Iraq.

DEBBIE

Vietnam? Iraq?

GODWIN

You'll know about Vietnam soon.

In three years, we'll have over half a million troops there. About 58,000 of them will come home in boxes.

                    DEBBIE
Dear God!

                    GODWIN
Debbie, I need you to pay attention. In about 20
minutes, all the cops upstairs will head
downtown to see Oswald paraded for the press.

That's when I'll leave.

                    DEBBIE
Shouldn't we try to stop Ruby?

Godwin spreads his palms.

                    GODWIN
I can't walk into a police station and expect to
walk out again.

                    DEBBIE
You make the future sound so bleak.

Godwin stands on tiptoe and gently pulls Debbie to him.

                    GODWIN
My wife... died very young. You look so much
like her that...

They KISS. A LENGTHY kiss of LONGING, of PARTING.

When she pulls away, Debbie looks at Godwin and for the first time SEES a
MAN, not a boy.

                    GODWIN
Your own future is what YOU make it.

INT. OLD RED COURTHOUSE - DAY

The door under the staircase opens and Godwin peeps out.

He watches people leaving the courthouse.

Coulter, Ficke and Lundgren exit though a revolving door.

He steps into the small space and holds up the Device. He checks the battery.
He pushes the lever once. Then again.

SFX: The scene SHIMMERS, WARPS, then FREEZES.

Dust motes dance in a sunbeam. Godwin is GONE.

EXT. OLD RED COURTHOUSE - DAY

Carrying the jack, Debbie hurries down the steps just in time to see her car TOWED away. As the tow truck turns the corner, Debbie drops the jack and sprints after it.

She rounds the corner onto Houston Street, steps into the street and holds up her BADGE.

A CAR BRAKES to a halt. Debbie jumps into the passenger seat.

INT. COMMANDEERED CAR - CONTINUOUS

The driver, a MIDDLE AGED WOMAN, stares at her, dumbfounded.

> DEBBIE
> Take me to police headquarters!

The driver pulls away without looking in her mirror.

EXT. HOUSTON STREET - DAY

A PICKUP SIDESWIPES the car, driving it into the curb. A column of white steam rises from the hood. Debbie jumps out and runs to a bus at the corner. She pounds on the door.

INT. BUS - CONTINUOUS

Waving her badge, Debbie confronts the driver.

> DEBBIE
> Take me to police headquarters!

> DRIVER
> Sorry, officer. I'm out of service.

> DEBBIE
> I'm commandeering this vehicle. Take me to
> Dallas PD headquarters!

The driver turns the IGNITION switch. A faint CLICK is heard.

> DRIVER
> Like I said, out of service.

EXT. HOUSTON STREET - DAY

Debbie sprints down the street, turns a corner and sees a crowd and cars double-parked outside the police station.

EXT. DALLAS PD HEADQUARTERS - DAY

Holding her badge aloft, she tries to push through the crowd. Her way is blocked by a burly sergeant.

> SERGEANT
> Nobody in or out.

> DEBBIE
> I'm a police officer.

> SERGEANT
> Some peckerhead just shot Oswald.
> This is a crime scene.

DAZED, Debbie retreats and sits on the curb, oblivious to the frenzied activity on the street.

EXT. CALIFORNIA INSTITUTE OF TECHNOLOGY - DAY

Head down, lost in thought, Godwin strides across the campus on a spring day -- and almost COLLIDES with Professor Wieman.

> WIEMAN
> Robert!

Godwin looks up and is BLANK is for a moment.

> WIEMAN (CONT'D)
> When did you return?

> GODWIN
> Wolfie! Sorry. Wool-gathering, as usual. I'm just
> back, actually.

                              WIEMAN
          How's that book coming?

                              GODWIN
          Book?

                              WIEMAN
          The time-travelling professor?

                              GODWIN
          I can't seem to find an ending.

          My protagonist fails at everything and returns
          with terminal weltschmerz.

          He's ready to destroy his time machine.

                              WIEMAN
          Can it wait until after lunch?

                              GODWIN
          I suppose I could use a good meal. Anything but
          Tex-Mex.

                              WIEMAN
          I'm on my way over to the Athenaeum.

They walk across the campus, then climb a FLIGHT of STEPS.

Suddenly Godwin stops, then wavers, his face ASHEN.

                              WIEMAN (CONT'D)
          Robert! What's wrong.

                              GODWIN
          (wheezing) Can't catch my breath.

Clutching his chest, Godwin falls to the step.

INT. HOSPITAL EMERGENCY ROOM - DAY

ADMINISTERING CPR, PARAMEDICS HUSTLES an ASHEN Godwin down the
corridor, trailed by Wieman.

An E.R. DOCTOR APPEARS in the corridor as the gurney approaches the
OPERATING ROOM.

                    PARAMEDIC
          Patient is comatose and unresponsive. Pulse is
          faint, vitals falling off the chart.

                    WIEMAN
          Is he going to be all right?

                    E.R. DOCTOR
          You'll have to wait outside.

INT. OPERATING ROOM - CONTINUOUS

Bedlam. Nurses scurry. A RADIOLOGIST peers at an X-Ray image of a heart on
a light box.

                    E.R. DOCTOR
          He's on life support—but look at his superior
          vena cava! And that right ventricle! We should
          just call it.

                    RADIOLOGIST
          The chief is down the hall. Let him make the
          call.

                    E.R. DOCTOR
          Then don't page him -- *bring* him!

INT. INTENSIVE CARE UNIT - NIGHT

Godwin is hooked to a dozen machines with digital displays.

INT. E.R. WAITING ROOM - DAY

Wieman dozes in a chair. A tall, handsome cardiologist, grey curls peeking out
from beneath his surgical cap, appears.

                    CARDIOLOGIST
          (slight DRAWL) Professor Wieman? You're
          Professor Godwin's colleague?

Wieman opens his eyes and slowly gets to his feet.

                    WIEMAN
          How is he?

                    CARDIOLOGIST
Resting. Lucky I was in the building. If one of
the residents had taken a crack at him...

                    WIEMAN
Can I see him?

                    CARDIOLOGIST
Give him a few days.

INT. ICU - DAY

Still wired to monitors but sitting up, Robert sips juice as the cardiologist
enters.

                    CARDIOLOGIST
How're we feeling today, Professor?

                    GODWIN
(SIGHS) Like we was rode hard and put away
wet.

                    CARDIOLOGIST
Sounds like you've been to Texas.

                    GODWIN
In my second childhood.

                    CARDIOLOGIST
You'll feel better soon.

                    GODWIN
Am I going to be one of these walking invalids?

                    CARDIOLOGIST
Not a chance. I rebuilt your pump--you're sore
now, but a few more days and you'll be most
good as new.

                    GODWIN
Guess I'll have to name my first-born after you,
Doctor...?

                    CARDIOLOGIST
Schmidlap. Austin Schmidlap.

                    GODWIN
          (SLOWLY) Your name's *really* Austin
          Schmidlap?

The cardiologist points to his name tag.

                    CARDIOLOGIST
          Like Lucy always says, would a real Texan make
          up a name like that?

Godwin's eyes ARE WIDE with amazement.

The bank of monitors begin to BEEPING wildly.

                    CARDIOLOGIST (CONT'D)
          I say something wrong, professor?

                    GODWIN
          Lucy is your wife?

                    CARDIOLOGIST
          My mother.

The beeping S L O W S.

                    GODWIN
          Dr. Schmidlap. Austin. Who taught you to swim?

                    CARDIOLOGIST
          Well, that's kind of a funny story. When I was
          five, we lived in Dallas, and I had this
          babysitter—he made the best omelets —

                    GODWIN
          Austin!
          (A LONG BEAT)
          (robot's voice) I. Was. A. Time. Traveler. From.
          The. 21st Century. I. Came. To. Save. The.
          World. From. A. Great. Tragedy.

Austin stares, unable to speak. Tears roll down his cheeks.

                    CARDIOLOGIST

          Bobby?

                    GODWIN
          Please tell me that Lucy is still alive.

Slowly, Austin nods, yes.

— THE END —

ABOUT THE AUTHORS

<u>Marvin J. Wolf</u>
Over a career spanning forty years, Marvin J. Wolf has written for television and authored many nonfiction works, including bestsellers FALLEN ANGELS, FAMILY BLOOD: THE TRUE STORY OF THE YOM KIPPUR MURDERS, and WHERE WHITE MEN FEAR TO TREAD.

<u>Larry Mintz</u>
A product of the Bronx, Larry Mintz is the writer/producer of such classic sitcoms as "Step By Step," "Sanford and Son, "Married With Children," "Family Matters" and "What's Happening," and co-writer of several feature films, including "Angels In The Outfield," "Till Death Do Us Part," and "Teen Angel." He also collaborated with Marvin J. Wolf on "Ladies Night," a made for television feature film.

Also By Marvin J. Wolf

NONFICTION

Family Blood

Fallen Angels

Rotten Apples

Perfect Crimes

Buddha's Child

Beating The Odds

Where White Men Fear To Tread

FICTION

For Whom The Shofar Blows